LAST OF THE GODS

Before Kirk's unbelieving eyes, the body of the man-sized being began to rise, taller, taller, taller. He towered twelve feet above them—and still grew higher. He was now a good eighteen feet in stature, a colossus of mingled beauty and rage. As the black brows drew together in fury, there came a deafening crash of thunder. The translucent light in the temple went dim, streaks of lightning piercing its darkness. Thunder rolled again. Around the temple's columned walls far above him, Kirk could see that lightning spears were gathering about the great head in a dazzling nimbus of flame.

Crowned with fire, Apollo said, "Welcome to Olympus, Captain Kirk!"

And this mighty being, having cut Kirk off from the **Enterprise** completely, demanded only one thing—absolute and unending worship.

A new collection of tales of high adventure from the great TV series.

STAR TREK 7

STAR TREK

JAMES BLISH

Based on the exciting
television series created
by GENE RODDENBERRY

BANTAM BOOKS · TORONTO · NEW YORK · LONDON

A NATIONAL GENERAL COMPANY

RLI: VLM 8 (VLR 7-9)
IL 7-up

STAR TREK 7
A Bantam Book published July 1972

Published simultaneously in the United States and Canada

Bantam Books are published by Bantam Books, Inc., a National
General company. Its trade-mark, consisting of the words "Bantam
Books" and the portrayal of a bantam, is registered in the United
States Patent Office and in other countries. Marca Registrada.
Bantam Books, Inc., 666 Fifth Avenue, New York, N.Y. 10019.

PRINTED IN THE UNITED STATES OF AMERICA

WHO MOURNS FOR ADONAIS?

(Gilbert A. Ralston and Gene L. Coon)

All heads in the *Enterprise* bridge turned as the elevator door opened.

Kirk made a bet with himself: it was Lieutenant Carolyn Palamas with her report on those marblelike fragments they'd beamed up from the dead planet in the Cecrops cluster. He won the bet. She handed him some stapled sheets and he said, "Thank you," his eyes carefully averted from the girl's lustrous slate-gray ones.

Supreme beauty, he'd decided, could be a cruel liability to a woman. The stares it attracted set her apart. And he didn't want Carolyn Palamas to feel set apart. If she was the owner of copper-glorious hair and those slate-gray eyes, she was also a new member of his crew and a highly competent archeologist. She'd been stopping traffic since the day she was born. Well, he wasn't adding his gapes to the quota. He said, "Continue with standard procedures for Pollux Four, Lieutenant."

Dr. McCoy appeared to share his defensiveness toward the traffic-stopper. "You look tired, Carolyn," he said.

"I worked all night on my report," she said.

1

"There's nothing like a cup of coffee to buck you up," Scott said. "Want to join me in one, Carolyn?"

She smiled at him. "Just let me get my chemicals back into the lab cabinet first." She left the bridge and Kirk said, "Could you get that excited over a cup of coffee, Bones?"

"I'm in love with her," Scott said briefly. As he hastened after her, a slight frown pulled at McCoy's brows. "I'm wondering about that, Jim."

"Scotty's a good man," Kirk said.

"He thinks he's the right man for her, but *she*—" McCoy shrugged. "Emotional analysis of this love goddess of ours shows up strong drives for wifehood and motherhood. She's all woman, Jim. One of these days the bug will find her and off she'll go—out of the Service."

"I'd hate to lose a good officer, but I never fight nature, Bones."

Chekov spoke from his station near Kirk's command chair. "Entering standard orbit around Pollux Four, sir."

On the screen Pollux Four had already appeared, not unearthlike. Continents, seas, clouds.

"Preliminary reports, Mr. Spock?"

"Class M, Captain." Spock didn't turn from his mounded computer. Kirk, his eyes on the screen, saw the planet, rotating slowly, come into closer focus. He heard Spock say, "Nitrogen-oxygen atmosphere, sir. Sensor readings indicate no life-forms. Approximate age four billion years. I judge no reason for contact. In all respects quite ordinary."

Kirk pushed a button. "Cartographic section, implement standard orders. All scanners automatic. All—"

"Captain!" shouted Sulu. "On scanner twelve!"

Something had suddenly come between them and the planet—something formless and so transparent Kirk could see the stars through it. It was rapidly growing in size.

"What in the name of . . ." McCoy fell silent.

"Mr. Sulu," Chekov said, "am I seeing things?"

"Not unless I am, too," Sulu said. "Captain, that thing is a giant hand!"

Kirk didn't speak. On the screen the amorphous mass had begun to differentiate itself into five gigantic fingers, into a palm, the hint of a massive wrist extending down and out of the viewer's area. "Readings, Mr. Spock." His voice was toneless. "Is it a hand?"

"No, Captain. Not living tissue."

"A trick then? A magnified projection?"

"Not a projection, sir. A field of energy."

"Hard about!" Kirk ordered briskly. "Course 230 mark 41."

The palm now dominated the screen, its lines deeply shadowed valleys, the huge, contrasting mounds of its construction simulating the human-size mounds of a human palm. The valleyed lines deepened, moving—and Chekov cried, "It means to grab us!"

For the first time Spock turned from his computer to look at the viewer. "Captain, if it's a force field—"

"All engines reverse!" Kirk shouted.

Lights flickered. Shudders shook the starship. Strained metal screamed. Bridge seats tumbled their occupants to the floor. Scrambling up to wrestle with his console, Sulu grasped it with both hands as he fought to pull it backward. "The helm won't answer, Captain! We can't move!"

Scott had rushed in from the elevator; and Kirk, regaining his chair, addressed Uhura. "Lieutenant, relay our position and circumstances to Star Base Twelve immediately. Report that the *Enterprise* has been stopped in space by an unknown force of some kind." He swung his chair around to Sulu. "Mr. Sulu, try rocking the ship. Full impulse forward, *then* back."

"Damage report coming in, Captain," said Uhura. "Situation under control. Minor damage stations three, seven and nineteen."

"Mr. Sulu?"

"Applying thrust, sir."

The ship vibrated. "No results, Captain. We're stuck tight."

Kirk glanced at the screen. The palm still owned it; and stars still shone through it. He looked away from it. "Status, Mr. Spock?"

"The ship is almost totally encircled by a force

3

field, sir. It resembles a conventional force field but of unusual wavelengths. Despite its likeness to a human appendage, it is not living tissue. It is energy."

"Thank you, Mr. Spock. Forward tractor beams, Mr. Sulu—and adjust to repel."

"Aye, aye, sir."

"Activate now!"

The ship quivered, groaning. "Ineffective, sir," Sulu said. "There doesn't seem to be anything to push against."

Spock spoke. "I suggest we throw scanner twelve on the main viewing screen, Captain."

"Do so, Mr. Spock."

The palm slid away. In its place, nebulous, still transparent, the features of a great face were shaping themselves into form on the screen. Silence was absolute in the bridge of the *Enterprise*. The immense face could be seen now, whole. But its immensity struck Kirk as irrelevant. It was an intensely masculine face; and whomever it belonged to was the handsomest male Kirk had ever seen in his life. The dark eyes were fixed on the ship. Diademed with stars, the brow, the nose and mouth conformed to convey an impression of classic beauty, ageless as the stars.

The voice that came from the screen suited the face.

"The aeons have passed, and what has been written has come about. You are welcome here, my beloved children. Your home awaits you."

Kirk shook his head as though to clear his ears of the deep organ tones reverberating through the bridge. He tore his gaze from the screen to address Uhura. "Response frequencies, Lieutenant."

"Calculated, sir. Channel open."

He pulled the mike to him. "This is Captain James T. Kirk of the *USS Enterprise*. Please identify yourself."

The request was ignored. "You have left your plains and valleys to make this bold venture," said the voice. "So it was from the beginning. We shall remember together. We shall drink the sacramental wine. The pipes shall call again from the woodlands. The long wait is ended."

4

The words had the sound of an incantation. Kirk said, "Whatever you are, whoever you are, are you responsible for stopping my ship?"

"I have caused the wind to withdraw from your sails."

"Return it," Kirk said. "Then we'll talk. You seem unwilling to identify yourself, but I warn you we have the power to defend ourselves. If you value your safety, release this ship!"

The lips moved in an approving smile. "You have the old fire. How like your fathers you are. Agamemnon . . . Achilles . . . Trojan Hector . . ."

"Never mind the history lesson. Release this ship or I'll—"

The smile faded. "You will obey—lest I close my hand—thus—"

The ship rocked like a toy shaken by a petulant child.

"External pressure building up, Captain," Scott called from his station. "Eight hundred GSC and mounting."

"Compensate, Mr. Scott."

"Pressure becoming critical, sir. One thousand GSC. We can't take it."

Savagely Kirk swung around to the screen. "All right, whatever you're doing, you win. Turn it off."

"That was your first lesson. Remember it," the voice said. The sternness on its face was replaced by a smile radiant as sunlight. "I invite you and all your officers to join me, Captain. Don't bring the one with the pointed ears. Pan is a bore. He always was."

Kirk said hastily, "Take it easy, Mr. Spock. We don't know what we're up against."

"Hasten, children," urged the voice. "Let your hearts prepare to sing."

"Well, Bones, ready for the concert?"

"Is that wise, Jim?"

"It is if we want a ship instead of a crushed eggshell."

Kirk got up to join his First Officer at the computer station. "You're in command, Mr. Spock. Get all labs working on the nature of the force holding us here. Find a way to break clear."

5

"Acknowledged, sir. Beam-down?"

"Yes, Mr. Spock."

The party materialized among olive trees. Ahead of them on a grassy knoll stood a small edifice of veinless marble. It was fronted by six fluted columns of the stone, lifting to capitals that flowered into graceful curves. Above them rose the white temple's architrave, embossed with sculptured figures. They looked ancient but somehow familiar. A semi-circled flight of steps led upward and into the structure.

As Chekov and Scott moved into position beside him, Kirk said, "Maintain readings on tricorders. That goes for everybody."

Behind him, unusually pale, Carolyn Palamas edged nearer to McCoy. "What am *I* doing here, Doctor?"

Unslinging his tricorder, McCoy said, "You're the student of ancient civilizations. This seems to be one. We'll need all the information you've got about it." He moved on to follow Kirk, adding, "The Captain will want us with him when he enters that door."

There was no door. They found themselves at once in a peristylelike open space. At its far end a dais made a pediment for a carved throne of the same spotless marble. There were benches of marble, a table that held a simple repast of fruit and wine. From somewhere came the sound of pipes, sweet, wild, pagan. On a bench beside the table sat a man-size being. Kirk had seen some good-looking men in his life, but this male, human or non-human, was in a class of his own. His face held the same agelessly classic beauty as the huge image of the *Enterprise* screen. A thigh-length garment was clasped to his sun-browned, smoothly muscular shoulders. Beside him lay a lyre. He rose to his tall six-foot two-inch height and walked to meet them.

"My children, greetings. Long, long have I waited for this moment."

His youth should have made the term "children" absurd. It didn't. He could get away with it, Kirk thought, because of the dignity. The whole bearing of the creature exuded it.

6

Low-voiced, he said, "Bones, aim your tricorder at him."

"Ah, the memories you bring of our lush and beautiful Earth!" The being flung up his arms as though invoking the memories. "Its green meadows . . . its blue skies . . . the simple shepherds and their flocks on the hills . . ."

"You know Earth?" Kirk asked. "You've been there?"

The white teeth flashed in the radiant smile. "Once I stretched out my hand—and the Earth trembled. I breathed upon it—and spring returned."

"You mentioned Achilles," Kirk said. "How do you know about him?"

"Search back into your most distant memories, those of the thousands of years that have passed . . . and I am there. Your fathers knew me and your fathers' fathers. I am Apollo."

It was insanely credible. The temple . . . the lyre. Apollo had been the patron god of music. And the speech of this being was marked by an antique cadence, an almost superhuman assurance. There was also his incomparable symmetry of body and gesture.

Chekov broke the spell. "Yes," he said, "and I am the Czar of all the Russias!"

"Mr. Chekov!"

"Sorry, Captain. I never met a god before."

"And you haven't now," Kirk said. "Your readings, Bones?"

"A simple humanoid. Nothing special."

"You have the manners of a satyr. You will learn." The remark was made abstractedly. The dark eyes had fixed on Carolyn Palamas. The creature stepped forward to lift her chin with his hand. Scott bristled and Kirk said, "Hold it, Scotty."

"Earth—she always was the mother of beautiful women. That at least is unchanged. I am pleased. Yes, we gods knew your Earth well . . . Zeus, my sister Artemis, Athene. Five thousand years ago we knew it well."

"All right," Kirk said. "We're here. Now let's talk.

Apparently, you're all alone. Maybe we can do something to help you."

"Help me? *You?* You will not help me. You will not leave this place." The tone was final. "Your transportation device no longer functions."

Kirk flipped open his communicator. There was no responding crackle. The being said casually, "Nor will that device work either, Captain." He paused. Just as casually, he added, "You are here to worship me as your fathers worshipped me before you."

"If you wish to play god by calling yourself Apollo, that is your business," Kirk said. "But you are not a god to us."

"I said," repeated the humanoid, "you shall worship me."

"You've got a lot to learn, my friend," Kirk retorted.

"And so have you! Let the lesson begin!"

Before Kirk's unbelieving eyes, the body of the man-size being began to rise, taller, taller, taller. He towered twelve feet above them—and still grew higher. He was now a good eighteen feet in stature, a colossus of mingled beauty and rage. As the black brows drew together in fury, there came a deafening crash of thunder. The translucent light in the temple went dim, streaks of lightning piercing its darkness. Thunder rolled again. Around the temple's columned walls far above him, Kirk could see that lightning spears were gathering about the great head in a dazzling nimbus of flame.

Crowned with fire, Apollo said, "Welcome to Olympus, Captain Kirk!"

Dazed, the *Enterprise* commander fought against the evidence of his senses. His reason denied the divinity of the being; but his eyes, his ears, insisted on its truth. Then he saw that a look of weariness, of pain, had appeared on Apollo's face. The massive shoulders sagged. He vanished.

It was McCoy who spoke first. "To coin a phrase—fascinating."

Kirk turned to the girl. "Lieutenant Palamas, what do you know about Apollo?"

She stared at him unseeingly. "What? . . . oh, Apollo.

He—he was the son of Zeus and Latona . . . a mortal woman. He was the god of light, of music, of archery. He—he controlled prophecy."

"And this creature?"

She had collected herself. "Clearly he has some knowledge of Earth, sir. His classic references, the way he speaks, his—his looks. They resemble certain museum sculptures of the god."

"Bones?"

"I can't say much till I've checked out these readings. He looks human, but of course that doesn't mean a thing."

"Whatever he is, he seems to control a remarkable technology," Chekov said.

"Power is what the thing controls," Scott said. "You can't pull off these tricks without power."

"Fine. But what power? Where does it come from?" Kirk's voice was impatient. "Scout around with your tricorders and see if you can locate his power source."

Scott and Chekov moved off and Kirk, his face grown thoughtful, turned to McCoy. "I wonder if five thousand years ago a race of—"

"You have a theory, Jim?"

"I'm considering one. What if—"

"Jim, look!"

Man-size again, Apollo was sitting on his marble throne.

"Come to me," he said.

They obeyed. Kirk spoke. "Mister—" he began. He hesitated, then plunged. "Apollo, would you kindly tell us what you want from us? Omitting, if you please, all Olympian comments?"

"I want from you what is rightfully mine. Your loyalty, your tribute and your worship."

"What do you offer in exchange?"

The dark eyes brooded on Kirk's. "I offer you human life as simple and pleasureful as it was those thousands of years ago on our beautiful Earth so far away."

"We're not in the habit of bending our knees to everyone we meet with a bag of tricks."

"Agamemnon was one such as you. And Hercules. Pride, hubris." The deep voice was somber with memory. "They defied me, too—until they felt my wrath."

Scott had rejoined Kirk in time to hear this last exchange. "We are capable of some wrath ourselves," he said hotly.

"I have four hundred and thirty people on my ship up there," Kirk said, "and they—"

"They are mine," said Apollo. "To cherish or destroy. At my will."

Carolyn suddenly broke in. "But why? What you've said makes no sense."

The dark eyes veered from Kirk's to linger on the cloud of copper-glorious hair. "What is your name?"

"Lieutenant Palamas."

"I mean your *name*."

She glanced at Kirk as though for help. "Carolyn."

"Yes." Apollo leaned forward on the throne. "When she gave you beauty, Aphrodite was feeling unusually generous. I have a thousand tales to tell you. We shall speak together, you and I, of valor and of love."

"Let her alone!" Scott cried.

"You protest?" Apollo was amused. "You risk much, mortal."

Scott whipped out his phaser. "And so do you!"

With a lithe movement, Apollo was on his feet. He extended a finger at the phaser. A blue-hot flame leaped from it—and Scott yelled in pain. He dropped the weapon, recoiling.

Kirk bent to pick it up, but Chekov had already retrieved it. The phaser was a lump of melted metal. Chekov handed it to Kirk. It was still hot to the touch.

"Quite impressive." The respect in Kirk's voice was genuine. "Did you generate that force internally?"

"Captain!" shouted Chekov. "The phasers—all of them!"

Kirk withdrew his from his belt. It had been fused into the same mass of useless metal.

"None of your toys will function."

Apollo dismissed the subject of the ruined phasers by stepping from his white throne. He strode over to Carolyn to search the slate-gray eyes with his. "Yes," he said, "the Cyprian was unusually generous to you. But the bow arm should be bare . . ."

He touched her uniform. Its stuff thinned into soft golden folds. They lengthened to her feet. She was gowned in a robe of flowing archaic Greek design that left one white shoulder naked. Golden sandals had replaced her shoes. Wonderingly, she whispered, "It—it is beautiful."

"You are beautiful," he said. "Come."

"She's not going with you!" Scott shouted. He took an angry step toward them—and was slammed against a marble bench. McCoy ran to him.

"That mortal must learn the discipline of my temple," Apollo said. "So must you all." He had Carolyn's hand in his. "But you—you come with me."

Kirk made a move and the girl shook her head. "It's all right, Captain."

The sunlight smile was for her. "Good," Apollo said. "Without fear. You are fit." A radiance suddenly enveloped them. Their figures were absorbed by it. They disappeared.

McCoy called to Kirk. "Scotty's stunned. He'll come around. But the girl, Jim—I'm not sure at all it was wise to let her go off like that. Whatever this Apollo is, we'd better be careful in dealing with him."

"He'd have been hard to stop," Kirk said. "Scotty tried."

"It's his moods that worry me. You've seen how capricious he is. Benevolent one moment, angry the next. If she says one displeasing thing to him, he could kill her."

"Yes, he could." Kirk turned to Chekov. "Mr. Chekov, continue your investigations. You all right, Scotty?"

Leaning against McCoy's shoulder, the engineer shook his head dazedly. "I don't know. I'm tingling all over . . . a kind of inside burning. Did he take her with him?"

"So it would seem, Scotty."

"Captain, we've got to stop him! He wants her! The way he looks at her—"

"Mr. Scott, the Lieutenant volunteered to go with

11

him, hopefully to find out more about him. I understand your concern—but she's doing her job. It's time you started doing yours. We've got to locate the source of his power. You have a tricorder. Use it. One thing more. I want no more unauthorized action taken against him. I don't want you killed. That's an order."

Sullenly Scott stumbled away after Chekov and McCoy said, "Scotty doesn't believe in gods, Jim."

"Apollo could have been one though—once."

"Is *that* your theory?"

"Bones, suppose a highly sophisticated group of humans achieved space travel five thousand years ago. Suppose they landed on Earth near the area around the Aegean Sea. To the simple shepherds and tribesmen of primitive Greece wouldn't they have seemed to be gods? Especially if they were able to alter their shapes at will and command great energy?"

McCoy stared. Then he nodded soberly. "Like humans, occasionally benevolent, occasionally vindictive. Maybe you've got something. But I certainly wish that love-goddess girl were safely back on the *Enterprise*."

Under the golden sandals of the love-goddess girl, the grass of the olive-groved glade was soft. "A simple humanoid" was how Dr. McCoy had defined the man who strolled beside her. Birds threaded the air she breathed with melody. Her hand felt very small in his. He lifted it to his lips—and they were as warm as human lips. Above the bird song, she could hear the plashing of a waterfall. Vaguely Carolyn Palamas thought, "I am both afraid and not afraid. How is it possible to feel two such different feelings at once?"

"I have known other women," he said. "Mortals . . . Daphne, Cassandra. None were so lovely as you. You fear me?"

"I—don't know. It isn't every day a girl is flattered by—"

"A god? I do not flatter."

She reached for another subject. "How do you know so much of Earth?"

"How do you remember *your* home? Earth was so

dear to us, it remains forever a shrine. There were laughter, brave and goodly company—love."

"You are alone, so alone," she said. "The others—where are they? Hera, Hermes, your sister Artemis?"

"They returned to the stars on the wings of the wind," he said.

"You mean they died?"

"No. We gods are immortal. It was the Earth that died. Your fathers turned away from us until we were only memories. A god cannot survive as a memory. We need awe, worship. We need love."

"You really consider yourself to be a god?"

He laughed. "It's a habit one gets into. But in a real sense we were gods. The power of life and death was ours. When men turned from us, we could have struck down from Olympus and destroyed them. But we had no wish to destroy. So we came back to the stars again."

A note of infinite sadness entered his voice. "But those we had to leave behind, those who had loved us were gone. Here was an empty place without worship, without love. We waited, all of us, through the endless centuries."

"But you said the others didn't die."

"Hera went first. She stood before the temple and spread herself upon the wind in a way we have . . . thinner and thinner until only the wind remained. Even for gods there is a point of no return." He paused. Then he turned her around to face him.

"Now you have come," he said.

A breeze stirred the grass at her feet. The urgency in his eyes was familiar to the traffic-stopper. But in his it seemed uniquely moving. Abruptly she had a sense of imminent glory or catastrophe.

"I knew you would come to the stars one day. Of all the gods, I knew. I am the one who waited. I have waited for you to come and sit by my side in the temple. Why have you been so long? It has been . . . so lonely."

She didn't speak. "Zeus," he said, "took Latona, my mother. She was a mortal like you. He took her to care for, to guard, to love—thus . . ."

13

His arms were around her. She whispered, "No—no, please, not now. I—I feel you are most kind and your—your loneliness is a pain in my heart. But I don't know. I—"

"I have waited five thousand years."

He kissed her. She pulled back; and he released her at once. "I will leave you for a little to compose yourself. The temple is not far." He stooped to brush the burnished hair with his lips before turning to stride up the swell of the glade. She watched him go. A sob broke from her; and she covered her face with her hands. Glory—or catastrophe. Who could know which lay in wait? The bird song had sunk into silence and shadows were lengthening through the leaves of the olive trees. She waited another moment before she climbed the gladed upswell that led back to the temple.

The *Enterprise* party was quartering the area before it with tricorders. As she emerged from the trees, Chekov was calling to Kirk. "There's a repeated occurrence of registrations, Captain. A regularly pulsating pattern of radiated energy."

She was glad Scott's attention was fixed on the ground. "I can detect the energy pattern, too, Captain. But I can't focus on it."

"Apollo seems able to focus on it, Mr. Scott. He taps that power. How?"

"The electric eel can generate and control energy without harm to itself," Chekov said. "And the dryworm of Antos—"

"Not the whole encyclopedia, please," McCoy begged.

"The Captain asked for complete information," Chekov said stiffly.

"Jim, Spock is contaminating this boy."

"Mr. Chekov, what you're suggesting is that Apollo taps a flow of energy he discharges through his own body," Kirk said.

"That would seem to be most likely, sir."

"But we don't *know* where the energy comes from! That's what we've got to find out if we're to cut off its source!"

14

"Number one on our 'things to do'," murmured McCoy.

"Is that all you can offer, Bones?"

"Yes, except for this finding. Your Apollo's got an extra organ in his gorgeous chest. I can't even make a guess at its function."

"An extra organ. Bones, is there any chance—"

"Captain!" Scott shouted.

Apollo had assumed shape and substance on the temple steps. Kirk walked up to him. "Where is Lieutenant Palamas?"

"She is well."

"That's not good enough—"

"She is no longer your concern, Captain Kirk."

"You blood-thirsty heathen, what have you done with her?" Scott cried.

Kirk's stern "No!" came too late. Scott, snatching up a stone, charged Apollo, headlong. The finger extended—and the blue-hot streak lashed from it. Heels over head, Scott was whirled through the air. He fell with a crash; and the rock in his hand rolled down the knoll.

"Well?" Kirk said.

McCoy was kneeling beside Scott's crumpled body. "Not so well, Jim. He's in deep shock."

Kirk glanced at Scott's white face. Blood was seeping from a gash near his mouth. He stood immobile for a long moment, half-seeing the injection McCoy was preparing. Then he whirled to stride up to the temple steps. "All right, Mr. Last of the Gods. You wanted worshippers? You've got enemies. From now on—"

The finger pointed directly at him. The blue-hot flash struck him directly in the chest. It didn't fade. It didn't waver. Kirk choked, hands groping at his heart. He spun around—and fell flat on his face into unconsciousness.

McCoy, instantly beside him, lifted an eyelid. "Two patients," he muttered to nobody. "Two damn fools."

From behind the tree whose trunk had sheltered her from Scott's notice, Carolyn burst out of the dismay that had benumbed her. She flew to the temple steps, crying wildly, "What have you done to them? What have you done?"

"They—needed discipline." Apollo spoke wearily.

She turned her back on him to run to the two stricken crew members. Kirk was climbing slowly to his feet, McCoy's arm about his shoulders. She knelt beside Scott to wipe the blood from his chin with her robe. He opened his eyes at her touch and smiled faintly at her. "What happened?" he said.

"You let your enthusiasm get the better of your pragmatism," McCoy told him dryly.

"I—I was going to separate his head from his ruddy neck," Scott said.

"And you disobeyed an order not to do it! When we get back to the ship, you'll report for a hearing, Mr. Scott!"

"She's—worth it, Captain."

"You're an officer of the Starfleet! Start acting like one! Besides, you stiff-necked thistlehead, you could have got yourself killed!"

Carolyn leaped to her feet, eyes blazing. "Apollo would not kill!"

Kirk stared at her. *"Women!"* he thought. "They'll believe anything's true if they want to believe it is true." He said icily, "Lieutenant, he very nearly has killed—and several times."

"He could—but he *didn't!* Captain, you've got to see! He doesn't want to hurt anyone. He's just—terribly lonely. Please try to understand. He's the god of light, of music. He wouldn't hurt us!"

Kirk gripped her shoulders. "What happened when he took you away?"

"We—just talked."

"What about?"

"Captain, I—"

Kirk's voice was hard as the temple's stone. "Answer me, Lieutenant. What he said may help us."

Her eyes sought the ground. "He—said there was a point of no return . . . even for gods. Of course he's not a god—but he is *not* inhuman!"

"He's not human, either," Scott said grimly.

16

"No!" she cried. "He is something greater than human, nobler!"

"Lieutenant, there are four hundred and thirty people on our ship and we're all in trouble."

"Oh, I know it, Captain! Don't you think I know it? I just don't know what—" She burst into tears.

"Go easy on her, Jim."

"Why? So she can play around with an exciting new romance?"

"A god is making love to her. That's strong stuff, Jim."

Kirk shook his head in irritation. "How do you feel, Scotty?"

"I can't move my left arm."

"You won't for a while. There's some neural damage to the arm, Jim. I could repair it if I had the facilities."

"One more reason why we have to get out of here." Kirk walked over to a log, kicked it aside and turned to beckon to McCoy. "Bones, listen. I've been trying to remember my Greek mythology. After expending energy its gods needed rest just as humans do. At any rate, I intend to assume they did."

"You think this Apollo is off somewhere recharging his batteries?"

"That's not so far-fetched. He's disappeared again, hasn't he? Why shouldn't he be resting after the show he put on? Remember he's maintaining a force field on the ship while he drains off energy down here. Point? If we can overwork him, wear him out, that just might do it."

"The trouble with overworking him is that it could get us all killed."

"Not if we can provoke him into striking one of us again. The energy drainage could make him vulnerable to being jumped by the rest of us."

"I still think we might all get killed."

"Bones, you're a pessimist. It's our only out. When he comes back, we'll try it. Cue Chekov in on the plan. Scotty's useless arm counts him out of any scramble. By the way, let's get him into the shade of the temple. It's hot in the sun."

But Carolyn Palamas had already assisted Scott into

17

the temple's coolness. She was easing him down on a bench. Kirk, following them, heard her say, "I am so sorry, Scotty."

"I'm not blaming you," Scott said heavily, his eyes on her face. He shoved himself up with his right arm. "Carolyn, you must not let yourself fall in love with him!"

"Do you think I *want* to?"

Kirk had had enough. He interrupted them. "You are the one to answer that question, Lieutenant. What is it exactly you *do* want? If you've pulled yourself together, I'd be glad to hear."

"Jim, he's recharged his batteries."

McCoy's warning was very quiet. Kirk spun around. Strong, glowing, glorious with health, Apollo was reclining against the side of his marble throne, chin on fist, the dark eyes on all of them, watchful.

"Come here," he said.

Kirk, McCoy and Chekov obeyed. "You are trying to escape me. It is useless. I know everything you mortals do."

"You know nothing about us mortals," Kirk said. "The mortals you know were our remote ancestors. It was they who trembled before your tricks. They do not frighten us and neither do you." He spoke with deliberate insolence. "We've come a long way in five thousand years."

"I could sweep you out of existence with a wave of my hand." The radiant smile flashed. "Then I could bring you back. I can give life and I can take it away. What else does mankind demand of its gods?"

"We find one sufficient," Kirk said.

Apollo sighed, bored. "No more debate, mortal. I offer you eternal joy according to the ancient way. I ask little in return. But what I ask for I shall have."

He leaned forward. "Approach me."

They didn't move. Instead, they turned their backs on him and strolled toward the temple entrance.

"I said *approach* me!"

"No." Kirk flung the word over his shoulder.

"You will gather laurel leaves! You will light the

ancient fires! You will slay a deer—and make your sacrifice to me!"

Kirk roared with laughter. "Gather laurel leaves? Listen to him!"

"It's warm enough without lighting fires!" shouted McCoy.

Chekov chuckled. "Maybe we should dance around a Maypole."

Apollo rose. "You shall reap the reward of this arrogance."

"Spread out. Get ready," Kirk said quietly. Then he turned, shouting, "We are tired of you and your phony fireworks!"

"You have earned this—"

Apollo had lifted an arm when Carolyn's *"No!"* came in a scream. "No, please, *no!* A father does not destroy his children! You are gentle! You love them! How can they worship you if you hurt them? Mortals make mistakes. You know us!"

"Shsssh," Kirk hissed. She didn't so much as glance at him. She was on her knees now before the throne. "Please—you know so much of love. Don't hurt them!"

The raised arm lowered. Apollo stepped from the dais and bent to lift her in his arms. Then he placed her on his throne. His hand on her neck, he turned to face them.

"She is my love of ten thousand years," he said. "In her name I shall be lenient with you. Bring the rest of your people down to me. They will need homes. Tell your artisans to bring axes."

Kirk's voice was acid with disappointment. "And you'll supply the sheep we herd and the pipes we'll play."

Apollo took Carolyn in his arms. The sunny radiance gathered around them. They dissolved into it—and were gone.

"Captain, we must *do* something!"

Kirk strode over to Scott's bench. "We *were* doing something until that girl of yours interfered with it! All right, she stopped him this time! How long do you think her influence will last?"

It was a question Carolyn was asking herself.

Gods were notoriously unfaithful lovers. Now the summer grass in the olive-groved glade was still green beneath her sandals. But autumn and winter? They would come in their seasons. Summer would pass . . . and when it went, she would know. Catastrophe—or glory. Now there was no knowing, no knowing of anything but the warmth of his arm around her shoulder.

"They are fools," he was saying. "They think they have progressed. They are wrong. They have forgotten all that gives life meaning—meaning to the life of gods or of mortals."

"They are my friends," she said.

"They will be with you," he said. "I will cause them to stay with you—with us. It is for you that I shall care for them. I shall cherish them and provide for them all the days that they live."

She was trembling uncontrollably. She wrung her hands to still their shaking. He took them in his.

"No dream of love you have ever dreamed is I," he said. "You have completed me. You and I—we are both immortal now."

His mouth was on hers. She swayed and his kiss grew deeper. Then her arms reached for his neck. "Yes, it is true," she whispered. "Yes, yes, yes . . ."

Kirk glanced at her sharply as she re-entered the temple.

"Lieutenant, where is he?"

She didn't answer; and Scott, raising his head painfully from his bench, saw her face. "What's happened to her? If he—"

She passed him to move on toward the throne. Her look was the absent look of a woman who has just discovered she is one. It was clear that the men of the *Enterprise* had ceased to exist for her.

"She can't talk," Scott said bewilderedly. "He's struck her dumb."

"Easy does it, Scotty," Kirk said. "She won't talk to you. You're too involved. But she'll talk to me."

"Want some assistance, Captain?" Chekov asked.

"How old are you, Ensign Chekov?"

"Twenty-two, sir."

"Then stay where you are," Kirk said. He walked over to the girl. "Are you all right, Lieutenant Palamas?"

She stepped down from the dais. "What?"

"I asked if you are all right."

"All right? Oh yes. I—am all right. I have a message for you."

"Sit down," Kirk said. "Here on this bench. Beside me—here."

She swallowed. "He—he wants us to live in eternal joy. He wants to guard . . . and provide for us for the rest of our lives. He can do it."

Kirk got up. "All right, Lieutenant, come back from where you are. You've got work to do."

"Work?"

"He thrives on love, on worship. They're his meat."

"He gives so much," she said. "He gives—"

"We can't give him worship. None of us, especially you."

"What?"

"Reject him. You must!"

"I love him," she said.

Kirk rubbed a hand up his cheek. "All our lives, here and on the ship, depend on you."

"No! Not on me. Please, not on me!"

"On you, Lieutenant. Accept him—and you condemn the crew of the *Enterprise* to slavery. Do you hear me? *Slavery!*"

The slate-gray eyes were uncomprehending. "He wants the best for us. And he is so alone, so . . . so gentle." Her voice broke. "What you want me to do would break his heart. How can I? How can I?" She burst into passionate weeping.

"Give me your hand, Lieutenant."

"What?"

He seized her hand. "Feel mine? Human flesh against human flesh. It is flesh born of the same time. The same century begot us, you and I. We are contemporaries, Lieutenant!"

All sympathy had left his voice. "You are to remember what you are! A bit of flesh and blood afloat in illimitable space. The only thing that is truly yours is

21

this small moment of time you share with a humanity that belongs to the present. That's where your duty lies. He is the past. His moment in time is not our moment. Do you understand me?"

The slate-gray eyes were anguished. But he sustained the iron in his face until she whispered, "Yes—I understand." She rose, left him, bent distractedly to pick up a tricorder; and half-turning, looked up at the temple's ceiling as though she were listening.

"He's—calling me," she faltered.

"I hear nothing," he said.

She didn't reply. The iron in his face was steel now. Desperate, he grabbed her shoulders. As he touched them, their bone, their flesh seemed to be losing solidity. She grew misty, fading. Kirk was alone with the echo of his own word "nothing".

Sinking down on the bench, he put his head in his hands. *Slavery.* It would claim all of them, McCoy, Scotty, Chekov. And up on the ship, they, too, would be enslaved to the whims of this god of the past. Sulu, Uhura, Spock . . .

"Spock here, Captain! *Enterprise* to Captain Kirk! *Enterprise* calling Captain Kirk! Come in, Captain!"

"I've gone mad," Kirk said to his hands. His useless communicator beeped again. "Communication restored, Captain! Come in, Captain. First Officer Spock calling Captain Kirk . . ."

"Kirk here, Mr. Spock."

"Are you all right, sir?"

"All right, Mr. Spock."

"We have pinpointed a power source on the planet that may have some connection with the force field. Is there a structure of some sort near you?"

Kirk had a crazy impulse to laugh. "Indeed there is, Mr. Spock. I'm in it."

"The power definitely emanates from there."

"Good. How are you coming with the force field?"

"Nuclear electronics believes we can drive holes through it by synchronization with all phaser banks. We aim the phasers—and there'll be gaps in the field ahead of them."

Kirk drew a deep lungful of air. "That ought to do

it, Mr. Spock. Have Sulu lock in every phaser bank we've got on this structure. Fire on my signal—but cut it fine. We'll need time to get out of here."

"I would recommend a discreet distance for all of you, Captain."

"Believe me, Mr. Spock, we'd like to oblige but we're not all together. One of us is hostage to the Greek god Apollo. This marble temple is his power source. I want to know where he is when we attack it. Kirk out."

"I seem to have lost touch with reality." McCoy was looking curiously at Kirk. "Or maybe you have. Was that Spock you were talking to on that broken communicator—or the spirit world?"

"Function has been restored to it. Don't ask me how. Ask Spock when you see him again. Now we have to get out of here. All phaser banks on the *Enterprise* are about to attack this place. I'll give you a hand with Scotty."

Scott said, "I won't leave, sir." Then his anxiety burst out of him. "Captain, we've got to wait till Carolyn comes back before you fire on the temple. We don't know what he'll do to her if he's suddenly attacked."

"I know," Kirk said. "We'll wait, Scotty."

As he arranged the paralyzed arm around his shoulder, he said, "That mysterious organ in the gorgeous chest, Bones—could it have anything to do with his energy transmissions?"

"I can't think of any other meaning it could have, Jim."

The gorgeous chest, its extra organ notwithstanding, had another meaning for Carolyn Palamas. Its existence had plunged her into the battle of her life. Walking beside her god in the olive-groved glade, her eyes were blank with the battle's torture. It centered itself on one thought alone. She must not let him touch her. If he touched her . . .

"You gave them my message," he said. "Were they persuaded?"

They'd said he was the source of mysterious power. He was not. He was the source of mysterious rapture. People, millions of them, shared her moment of time.

23

They crowded it with her. But not one of them could evoke the ecstasy this being of a different time could bring to birth in her just by the sound of his voice.

"*You* persuaded them," he said. "Who could deny you anything?"

His eyes were the night sky, starred. He caught her in his arms; and not for her soul's sake or humanity's either, could she deny him her mouth. She flung her arms around his neck, returned his kiss—and pushed him away.

"I must say that the way you ape human behavior is quite remarkable," she said. "Your evolutionary pattern must be—"

"My what?"

"I'm sure it's unique. I've never encountered any specimen like you before."

"Haven't you?" he said. Running laughter sparkled in the dark eyes as he reached for her again. She held herself rigid, tight, withdrawn. The sparkle flamed into anger. "I am Apollo! I have chosen you!"

"I have work to do."

"Work? *You?*"

"I am a scientist. My specialty is relics—outworn objects of the past." She managed a shaken laugh. "Now you know why I have been studying you." She unslung her tricorder, aiming it at him. "I'd appreciate your telling me how you stole that temple artifact from Greece."

He knocked the tricorder out of her hand. "You cannot talk like this! You love me! You think I do not know when love is returned to me?"

"You confuse me with a shepherd girl. I could no more love you than I could love a new species of bacteria." Lifting the hem of her golden robe, she left him to climb back up the gladed hill. Then he was beside her. Anguish struggled with fury in his face.

"Carolyn, what have you said to me? I forbid you to go! I command you to return to me!"

"I am dying," was what she thought. What she said was: "Is this rage the thunderbolt that dropped your frightened nymphs to their knees?"

An eternity passed. His hand fell from her shoulder.

24

Then a wild cry broke from him. He raised an arm and shook a fist at the sky. The air in the glade went suddently sultry, oppressive. The sun disappeared. A chill breeze fluttered her robe as she began to run up the glade's incline.

It did more than flutter Kirk's jacket. A fierce gust of wind blew it half off his shoulders. Under its increasing howl his communicator beeped feebly. "Spock, Captain. Sensors are reporting intense atmospheric disturbance in your area."

The sensors hadn't exaggerated. The clouds over Kirk's head darkened to a sickly, yellowish blackness that hid the glimmer of the temple's marble. It was cleaved by a three-pronged snake of lightning before it flooded in again. There followed a crack of thunder; and another lightning flash struck from the sky. Kirk heard the sound of splitting wood—and an olive tree not five feet away burst into flame. Grabbing his communicator, he shouted into it. "Stand by, phaser banks! Mr. Spock, prepare to fire at my signal!"

Scott rushed to him. "Captain, we've got to go and find her!"

"Here is where we stay, Mr. Scott. When he comes back—" The wind took the words from his mouth.

"What if he doesn't, sir?"

"We'll bring him back. When that temple is—"

There was no need to bring him back.

He was back. The God of Storms himself. He topped the olive trees. A Goliath of power, Apollo of Olympus had returned in his gigantic avatar. The great head was flung back in agony, the vast mouth open, both giant fists lifted, clenched against the sky. It obeyed him. It gave him livid lightning forks to hurl earthward and filled his mouth with rolling thunder. Leaves shriveled. The tree trunk beside Kirk began to smoke. Then it flared into fire—and the black sky gave its God of Storms the lash of rain.

Stumbling toward the temple, Carolyn Palamas screamed. The gale's winds tore at her drenched robe. She screamed again as the bush she clung to was whipped from the ground, its branches clawing at her face. Apollo had found her. He was all around her, the blaze of his eyes in the lightning's blaze, in the rain that streamed down her body, the wild cry of the wind in the ears he had kissed. The she saw him. The God of Storms stooped from his height above the trees to show her his maddened face. He brought it closer to her, closer until she shrieked, "Forgive me! Forgive me!—" and lay still.

"Captain, you heard her! She screamed!"

"Now, Mr. Spock," Kirk said into his communicator. The incandescing phaser beams struck the temple squarely in its central roof.

"No! No! No!"

The god who had appeared before the temple dwarfed it. He had unclenched his fists to spread his hands wide on his up-flung arms. Bolts of blue-hot fire streamed from his fingers.

"Oh, stop it, stop it, *please!"*

Carolyn, running to Apollo, halted. Behind him the temple was wavering, going indistinct. It winked out— and was gone.

She fell to her knees before the man-size being who stood in its place.

He spoke brokenly. "I would have loved you as a father his children. Did I ask so much of you?"

The grief-ravaged face moved Kirk to a strange pity. "We have outgrown you," he said gently. "You asked for what we can no longer give."

Apollo looked down at the girl at his feet. "I showed you my heart. See what you've done to me."

She saw a slight wind stir his hair. She kissed his feet—but she knew. The flesh under her lips, his body was losing substance. Kirk made no move; but he had noted that the arms were spreading wide.

"Zeus, my father, you were right. Hera, you were wise. Our time is gone. Take me home to the stars on the wind . . ." The words seemed to come from a great distance.

It was very still in the empty space before the ruined temple.

"I—I wish we hadn't had to do that," McCoy said.

"So do I, Bones." Kirk's voice was somber. "Every-

26

thing grew from the worship of those gods of Greece—philosophy, culture. Would it hurt us, I wonder, to gather a few laurel leaves?"

He shook his head, looking skyward.

There were only the sounds of a woman's sobbing and the drip of raindrops from olive trees.

McCoy, sauntering into the *Enterprise* bridge, strolled over to Kirk and Spock at the computer station.

"Yes, Bones? Somebody ill?"

"Carolyn Palamas rejected her breakfast this mornin."

"Some bug going around?"

"She's pregnant, Jim. I've just examined her."

"What?"

"You heard me."

"Apollo?"

"Yes."

"Bones, it's impossible!"

McCoy leaned an arm on the hood of the computer.

"Spock," he said, "may I put a question to this gadget of yours? I'd like to ask it if I'm to turn my Sickbay into a delivery room for a human child—or a god. My medical courses did not include obstetrics for infant gods."

THE CHANGELING

(John Meredyth Lucas)

The last census had shown the Malurian system, which had two habitable planets, to have a population of over four billion; and only a week ago, the *Enterprise* had received a routine report from the head of the Federation investigating team there, asking to be picked up. Yet now there was no response from either planet, on any channel—and a long-range sensor sweep of the system revealed no sign of life at all.

There could not have been any system-wide natural catastrophe, or the astronomers would have detected it, and probably even predicted it. An interplanetary war would have left a great amount of radioactive residue; but the instruments showed only normal background radiation. As for an epidemic, what disease could wipe out two planets in a week, let alone so quickly that not even a single distress signal could be sent out—and what disease could wipe out *all* forms of life?

A part of the answer came almost at once as the ship's deflector screens snapped on. Something was approaching the *Enterprise* at multi-warp speed: necessarily, another ship. Nor did it leave a moment's doubt about its intentions. The bridge rang to a slamming jar. The *Enterprise* had been fired upon.

"Shields holding, Captain," Scott said.

"Good."

"I fear it is a temporary condition," Spock said. "The shields absorbed energy equivalent to almost ninety of our photon torpedos."

"*Ninety,* Mr. Spock?"

"Yes, Captain. I may add, the energy used in repulsing that first attack has reduced our shielding power by approximately 20 percent. In other words, we can resist perhaps three more; the fourth one will get through."

"Source?"

"Something very small . . . bearing 123 degrees mark 18. Range, ninety thousand kilometers. Yet the sensors still do not register any life forms."

"Nevertheless, we'll try talking. They obviously pack more wallop than we do. Lieutenant Uhura, patch my audio speaker into the translator computer and open all hailing frequencies."

"Aye, sir . . . All hailing frequencies open."

"To unidentified vessel, this is Captain Kirk of the *USS Enterprise.* We are on a peaceful mission. We mean no harm to you or to any life-form. Please communicate with us." There was no answer. "Mr. Spock, do you have any further readings on the alien?"

"Yes, sir. Mass, five hundred kilograms. Shape, roughly cylindrical. Length, a fraction over one meter."

"Must be a shuttlecraft," Scott said. "Some sort of dependent ship, or a proxy."

Spock shook his head. "There is no other ship on the sensors. The object we are scanning is the only possible source of the attack."

"What kind of intelligent creatures could exist in a thing that size?"

"Intelligence does not necessarily require bulk, Mr. Scott."

"Captain, message coming in," Uhura said.

The voice that came from the speaker was toneless, inflectionless, but comprehensible. "*USS Enterprise.* This is Nomad. My mission is non-hostile. Require communication. Can you leave your ship?"

"Yes," Kirk said, "but it will not be possible to enter your ship because of size differential."

"Non sequitur," said Nomad. "Your facts are un-coordinated."

"We are prepared to beam you aboard our ship."

Kirk's officers, except for Spock, reacted with alarm at this, but Nomad responded, "That will be satisfactory."

"Do you require any special conditions, any particular atmosphere or environment?"

"Negative."

"Please maintain your position. We are locked on to your coordinates and will beam you aboard." Kirk made a throat-cutting gesture to Uhura, who broke the contact.

"Captain," Scott said, "you're really going to bring that thing in here?"

"While it's on board, Mr. Scott, I doubt very much if it will do any more shooting at us. And if we don't do what it asks, we're a sitting duck for it right now. Lieutenant Uhura, have Dr. McCoy report to the Transporter Room. Mr. Spock, Scotty, come with me."

The glowing swirl of sparkle that was the Transporter effect died, and Nomad was there, a dull metallic cylinder, resting in a horizontal position on the floor of the chamber. It was motionless, silent, and a little absurd. There were seams on its sides, indicating possible openings, but there were no visible ports or sensors.

Spock moved to a scanning station, then shook his head. "No sensor readings, Captain. It has some sort of screen which protects it. I cannot get through."

There was a moment's silence. Then McCoy said: "What do we do now? Go up and knock?"

As if in answer, the flat inflectionless voice of Nomad spoke again, now through the ship's intercom system. "Relate your point of origin."

Kirk said, "We are from the United Federation of Planets."

"Insufficient response. All things have a point of origin. I will scan your star charts."

Kirk thought about this for a moment, then turned to Spock. "We can show it as a closeup of our system. As

30

long as it has nothing to relate to, it won't know anything more important than it does now."

"It seems a reasonable course," Spock said.

"Nomad," Kirk told the cylinder, "If you would like to leave your ship, we can provide the necessary life-support systems."

"Non sequitur. Your facts remain uncoordinated."

"Jim," said McCoy, "I don't believe there's anyone in there."

"I contain no parasitical beings. I am Nomad."

"Och, it's a machine!" Scott said, brightening.

"Opinion, Mr. Spock?"

"Indeed, Captain, it is reacting quite like a highly sophisticated computer."

"I am Nomad. What is 'opinion'?"

"Opinion," Spock said, "is a belief, view or judgment."

"Insufficient response."

"What's your source of power?" Scott said.

"It has changed since the point of origin. There was much taken from the other. Now I focus cosmic radiation, and am perpetual."

Kirk drew Spock aside and spoke in a low voice. "Wasn't there a probe called Nomad launched from Earth back in the early two thousands?"

"Yes. It was reported destroyed. There were no more in the series. But if this *is* that probe—"

"I will scan your star charts now," Nomad said.

"We'll bring them."

"I have the capability of movement within your ship."

After a moment's hesitation, Kirk said, "This way. Scotty, get our shields recharged as soon as possible. Spock, Bones, come with me."

He led the way to the auxiliary control room, Nomad floating after him. The group considerably startled a crewman who was working there.

Spock crossed to the console. "Chart fourteen A, sir?"

Kirk nodded. The First Officer touched buttons quickly, and a view-screen lit up, showing a schematic chart of Earth's solar system—not, of course, to scale.

"Nomad," Kirk said, "can you scan this?"

"Yes."

"This is our point of origin. A star we know as Sol."

"You are from the third planet?"

"Yes."

"A planet with one large natural satellite?"

"Yes."

"The planet is called Earth?"

"Yes it is," Kirk said, puzzled.

An antenna slid from the side of the cylinder, swiveled, and centered upon him. He eyed it warily.

"Then," said Nomad, "you are the Creator—the Kirk. The sterilization procedure against your ship was a profound error."

"What sterilization procedure?"

"You know. You are the Kirk—the Creator. You programmed my function."

"Well, I'm not the Kirk," McCoy said. "Tell *me* what your function is."

The antenna turned to center on the surgeon. "This is one of your units, Creator?"

"Uh . . . yes, he is."

"It functions irrationally."

"Nevertheless, tell him your function."

The antenna retracted. "I am sent to probe for biological infestations. I am to destroy that which is not perfect."

Kirk turned to Spock, who was working at an extension of the library computer. "Biological infestations? There never was any probe sent out for that."

"I am checking its history," Spock said. "I should have a read-out in a moment."

Kirk turned back to Nomad. "Did you destroy the Malurian system? And why?"

"Clarify."

"The system of this star, Omega Ceti."

"Not the system, Creator Kirk, only the unstable biological infestation. It is my function."

"Unstable manifestation!" McCoy said angrily. "The population of two planets!"

"Doctor," Kirk said warningly. "Nomad, why do you call me Creator?"

"Is the usage incorrect?"

"The usage is correct," Spock put in quickly. "The Creator was simply testing your memory banks."

What, Kirk wondered, was Spock on to now? Well, best keep silent and play along.

"There was much damage in the accident," Nomad said.

Kirk turned toward the crewman, who had been listening with growing amazement. "Mr. Singh, come over here, please. Mr. Spock, Doctor, go to the briefing room. Nomad, I will return shortly. This unit, called Singh, will see to your needs."

There was no reaction from the cylinder. Kirk joined Spock and McCoy in the corridor. "Spock, you're on to something. What is it?"

"A Nomad probe was launched from Earth in August of the year 2002, old calendar. I am convinced that this is the same probe."

"Ridiculous," McCoy said. "Earth science couldn't begin to build anything with those capabilities that long ago."

"Besides," Kirk added, "Nomad was destroyed."

"Presumed destroyed by a meteor collision," Spock said. "I submit that it was badly damaged, but managed somehow to repair itself. But what is puzzling is that the original mission was a peaceful one." They had reached the briefing room, and the First Officer stepped aside to allow Kirk to precede him in. "The creator of Nomad was perhaps the most brilliant, though erratic, cyberneticist of his time. His dream was to make a perfect thinking machine, capable of independent logic. His name was Jackson Roykirk."

Light dawned. "Oho," Kirk said.

"Yes, Captain, I believe Nomad thinks you are Roykirk, and that may well be why the attack was broken off when you hailed it. It responded to your name, as well as its damaged memory banks permitted. While we were in Auxiliary Control, I programmed the computer to show a picture of the original Nomad on the screen here."

Spock switched on the screen. On it appeared, not a photograph, but a sketch. The size and shape indicated

33

were about the same as the present Nomad, but the design was somehow rougher.

"But that's not the same," McCoy said.

"Essentially it is, Doctor. But I believe more happened to it than just damage in the meteor collision. It mentioned 'the other'. The other *what* is still an unanswered question. Nomad was a thinking machine, the best that could be engineered. It was a prototype. However, the entire program was highly controversial. It had many powerful enemies in the confused and inefficient Earth culture of that time. When Jackson Roykirk died, the Nomad program died with him."

"But if it's Nomad," Kirk said, "what happened to alter its shape?"

"I think it somehow repaired the damage it sustained."

"Its purpose must have been altered. The directive to seek out and destroy biological infestations couldn't have been programmed into it."

"As I recall, it wasn't," McCoy said. "Seems to me it was supposed to be the first interstellar probe to seek out new life-forms—only."

"Precisely, Doctor," Spock said. "And somehow that programming has been changed. It would seem that Nomad is now seeking out *perfect* life-forms . . . perfection being measured by its own relentless logic."

"If what you say is true, Mr. Spock," Kirk said, "Nomad has effectively programmed itself to destroy all non-mechanical life."

"Indeed, Captain. We have taken aboard our vessel a device which, sooner or later, must destroy us."

"Bridge to Captain Kirk," said the intercom urgently.

"Here, Scotty."

"Sir, that mechanical beastie is up here on the bridge!"

"On my way." Kirk tried to remember whether or not he, as the misidentified "Creator," had given Nomad a direct order to stay in the auxiliary control room. Evidently not.

On the bridge Uhura, Scott and Sulu were on duty; Uhura had been singing softly to herself.

"I always liked that song," Sulu said.

As he spoke, the elevator doors opened, and Nomad emerged. It paused for a moment, antenna extended and swiveling, coming to rest at last on Uhura. It started towards her. (It was at this point that Scott had called for Kirk.)

"What is the meaning of that?" Nŏmad said. "What form of communication?"

Uhura stared; though she knew the device had been brought aboard, this was the first time she had actually seen it. "I don't know what you—oh, I was singing."

"For what purpose is this singing?"

"I don't know. Just because I felt like singing, felt like music."

"What is music?"

Uhura started to laugh—there was something inherently ludicrous about discussing music with a machine—but the laugh died quickly. "Music is a pleasant arrangement of musical tones—sound vibrations of various frequencies, purer than those used in normal speech, and with associated harmonics. It can be immensely more complex than what I was doing just then."

"What is its purpose?"

Uhura shrugged helplessly. "Just for enjoyment."

"Insufficient response," said the machine. A pencil of light shot out from it, resting a spot of light on her forehead, between and slightly above the eyes. "Think about music."

Uhura's face went completely blank. Scott lunged to his feet. "Lieutenant! Get away from that thing—"

The elevator doors opened and Kirk, Spock and McCoy entered. "Scotty, look out—" Kirk shouted.

Scott had already reached the machine and grabbed for it, as if to shove it out of the way. There was no movement or effect from the craft, but the engineer was picked up and flung with tremendous impact against the nearest bulkhead. Sulu leapt up to yank Uhura out of the beam of light.

Kirk gestured toward Scott and McCoy strode to him quickly and knelt. Then he looked up. "He's dead, Jim."

For a moment Kirk stood stunned and appalled.

35

Then fury rose to free him from his paralysis. "Why did you kill him?" he asked Nomad grimly.

"That unit touched my screens."

"That *unit* was my chief engineer." He turned to Uhura. "Lieutenant, are you all right? . . . Lieutenant! . . . Dammit, Nomad, what did you do to *her?*"

"This unit is defective. Its thinking was chaotic. Absorbing it unsettled my circuitry."

"The unit is a woman," Spock said.

"A mass of conflicting impulses."

Kirk turned angrily away. "Take Mr. Scott below."

"The Creator will effect repairs on the unit Scott?"

"He's dead."

"Insufficient response."

"His biological functions have ceased." Kirk was only barely able to control his rage and sorrow.

"If the Creator wishes," Nomad said emotionlessly, "I will repair the unit."

Startled, Kirk looked at McCoy, who said, "There's nothing I can do, Jim. But if there's a chance, it'll have to be soon."

"All right. Nomad, repair the unit."

"I require tapes on the structure."

Spock looked to McCoy. The surgeon said, "It'll need tapes on general anatomy, the central nervous system, one on the physiological structure of the brain. We'd better give it all the neurological studies we have. And tracings of Scotty's electro-encephalogram."

Spock nodded and punched the commands into the library computer as McCoy called off the requirements. "Ready, Nomad."

The device glided forward. A thin filament of wire extruded from it and touched a stud on the panel. Spock tripped a toggle and the computer whirred.

Then it was over and the filament pulled back into Nomad. "An interesting structure. But, Creator, there are so few safeguards built in. It can break down from innumerable causes, and its self-maintenance systems are unreliable."

"It serves me as it is, Nomad," Kirk said.

"Very well, Creator. Where is the unit Scott now?"

"Bones, take it to Sickbay." Kirk snapped a switch

and said into his mike, "Security. Twenty-four hour two-man armed surveillance on Nomad. Pick it up in Sickbay." He turned to Spock. "Nomad is operating on some kind of energy. We've got to find out what it is and put a damper on it. Surely it can't be getting much cosmic radiation inside the *Enterprise;* we're well shielded. Let's feed in everything that's happened so far to the computer, and program for a hypothesis."

"It seems the most reasonable course, Captain. But it won't be easy."

"Easy or not, I want it done. Get on it, Mr. Spock. Then report to me in Sickbay."

Scott's body lay upon the examination table, with Nomad hovering over it. McCoy and Nurse Christine Chapel stood beside it, while Kirk and the two Security guards stood near the wall. Nomad, antenna extended, was scanning the body and humming.

The nurse looked toward the body-functions panel. "No reaction, Doctor."

"Could have told you that without looking, Nurse."

Suddenly, a light appeared on the panel, and a dial began quivering. In time with its movements, there came a steady beeping sound, gradually picking up in speed and volume.

Scott's eyes opened and he looked up at the amazed group, frowning. While he stared back, Spock joined the others. "What are the lot of you staring at?" Scott demanded.

"I . . . don't . . . believe it," McCoy whispered.

Scott looked around, and spotting Nomad, its antenna retracted now, he sat up in alarm. "What am I doing here? How did I—That thing did something to Lieutenant Uhura—"

"She's being taken care of, Scotty," Kirk said.

"But sir, it's dangerous! It—"

"Take it easy, Scotty," McCoy said. "Now just lie down. I want to check you out."

"The unit Scott is repaired," Nomad said. "It will function as before if your information to me was correct."

"How about it, Bones? Can he go back to duty?"

37

"If you don't mind, I'll check him out first. A man isn't just a . . . a biological unit to be patched together."

"What did it do to me?" Scott said.

Suddenly, a wave of pure awe, as strong as any he had ever felt in his life, swept through Kirk. Back from the dead! Why, if—but he pushed speculation resolutely away for the time being. "Dr. McCoy will explain, Scotty."

"Nurse Chapel," McCoy said, "I want him prepared for a full physical exam."

"Yes, sir."

Kirk crossed the examination room toward Sickbay proper, where Uhura now was. "Nomad, come here."

The machine glided after him, followed by Spock and McCoy. Inside, the Communications Officer lay unmoving on a bed, in a hospital gown and covered by a blanket. She did not look at any of them.

"Can you repair her, Nomad?" Kirk demanded.

"No," said the machine.

"But you were able to restore Scott, who had much more extensive damage."

"That was simply physiological repair. This one's superficial knowledge banks have been wiped clean."

"Superficial? Be more specific."

"She still remembers her life experiences, but her memory of how to express them, either logically or in the illogic called music, or to act on them, has been purged."

"Captain, if that is correct," Spock said, "if her mind has not been damaged and the aphasia is that superficial, she could be taught again."

"Bones?"

"I'll get on it right away." McCoy swung on Nomad. "And despite the way you repaired Scotty, you ticking metal—"

"Does the Creator wish Nomad to wait elsewhere?" Spock broke in quickly.

"Yes. Guards! Nomad, you will go with these units. They will escort you to a waiting area. Guards, take it to the top security cell in the brig."

There was silence while the guards and the machine

went out. Then Spock said, "I interrupted you, Doctor, because Nomad would not have understood your anger. Its technical skill is great but it seems to react violently to emotion, even so non-specific an emotion as the enjoyment of music. It almost qualifies as a life-form itself."

Kirk glanced sharply at him. "It's all right to admire it, Mr. Spock, but remember it's a killer. We're going to have to handle it."

"I agree, Captain. It is a remarkable construction; it may well be the most advanced machine in the known galaxy. Study of it—"

"I intend to render it harmless, whatever it may take."

"You mean destroy it, Captain?"

"If it's necessary," Kirk said. "Get down to the brig with your equipment and run a full analysis of the mechanism. I want to know what makes that thing tick."

"Yes, sir."

The First Officer went out, and Kirk and McCoy returned to the examination room. Scott was still lying on the table. McCoy scanned the body functions panel slowly, and shook his head in disbelief.

"He checks out fine," he said. "Everything's normal."

"Then," Scott said, "can I get back to my engines, sir?"

Kirk glanced at McCoy, who nodded. "All right, Scotty."

"I hate to admit it," McCoy said as Scott swung off the table and left, "but Spock was right. Nomad is a remarkable machine."

"Just remember it kills as effectively as it heals, Bones . . . if I'm called, I'll be down in the brig."

The two Security guards, phasers in hand, stood outside the force-field door of the brig, which was on. Inside, Nomad floated, almost surrounded by an array of portable scanners, behind which was Spock, staring with disapproval at the machine. Nomad, its antenna out, "stared" back.

One of the guards switched off the screen to allow

Kirk to enter, then switched it on again. Kirk said, "What's the problem?"

"I have been unable to convince Nomad to lower its screens for analysis. Without its cooperation, I can do nothing."

Kirk studied the quietly humming machine. "Nomad, you will allow Spock to probe your memory banks and structure."

"This Spock is also one of your biological units, Creator?"

"Yes."

"This unit is different. It is well ordered. Interesting."

Under other circumstances, Kirk would have been amused to hear a machine applying Spock's favorite word to Spock himself, but the stakes were too great for amusement now. "Follow your orders, Nomad."

"My screens are down. You may proceed."

Spock set to work, very rapidly indeed, making settings, taking readings, making new settings. Within a few moments, he seemed to have found something which surprised him. He made another adjustment, and the machine he had been using promptly extruded a slip of paper, which he studied.

"Captain, I suggest we go out in the corridor for a private conference." They did so. "Sir, I have formed a partial hypothesis. But my information is insufficient and I have gleaned everything possible from the scanners. I must be allowed to question Nomad directly."

"Too dangerous."

"Captain, it moves only against imperfections. As you will recall, there is a Vulcan mind discipline which permits absolute concentration on one subject for a considerable period of time. If I were to use it—"

"And if your mind wandered for a moment, Nomad might just blast you out of existence. Right now it's safe in the brig."

"We do not know enough about it to know if it is 'safe' anywhere. If my hypothesis is correct, sir, we will at least be closer to understanding it. And control is not possible without understanding."

"All right," Kirk said, taking a phaser from one of the guards, "but I think I'll just keep this handy."

They went back in. Spock sat down on the cell bunk, for which the present prisoner had no use, and put his fingers to his temple. Kirk could almost hear his mind working.

"Nomad, my unit Spock will ask you certain questions. You will answer them as though I were asking them myself."

"Yes, Creator."

Silence. At last Spock said, "Nomad, there was an accident."

"There was an accident."

"You encountered the other."

"There was another. It was without direction. We joined."

"The other was not of the Earth. Its functions were other than yours." Spock held up the piece of paper, on which Kirk could see a drawing of what looked to be a space capsule of unfamiliar design. "I secured this design from your memory banks. Is this the other?"

"It is the other."

"Nomad, your memory banks were damaged by the accident. You took new directions from the other."

There was a buzz from the machine, and an antenna was aimed at Spock again. "Your statement is not recorded. You are in error."

"Logically, Nomad, you cannot prove I am in error, if your memory banks were damaged. You would have no way of knowing whether I speak the truth or not." Spock fell silent. The antenna retracted. "You acknowledge my logic. After meeting with the other, you had a new directive. Life-forms, if not perfect, are to be sterilized. Is this correct?"

"That is my programmed purpose."

"How much of the other did you assimilate?"

"Unrelated. Your question has no factual basis."

"Spock," Kirk said, "I think you're getting into deep waters. Better knock off."

Spock, unhearing, continued to stare at Nomad. The machine said: "There is error here. But if there was

41

damage to my memory cells, there can be no proof of error. I will consider it."

"Enough," Kirk said firmly. Signaling to the guards to drop the screen, he dragged Spock out. The Vulcan was still glassy-eyed. "Mr. Spock! Come out of it!"

Slowly Spock's eyes began to focus. "Yes, Captain?"

"Are you all right?"

"Quite all right, sir." He looked back into the brig. "Fascinating. I was correct. It did meet a completely alien probe in deep space."

"And they merged—or at least their purposes did."

"In effect. Nomad took the alien's prime purpose to replace that part of its own which had been destroyed. The alien was originally programmed to seek out and sterilize soil samples from various planets—possibly as a preliminary to colonization."

"Hmm. Spock, do you know what a changeling is?"

"Sir?"

"An ancient Earth legend. A changeling was supposed to be a fairy child left in place of a stolen human baby. The changeling took the identity of the human child."

"That would be a parallel if Nomad is actually the alien probe intact. But actually, its programming now is a combination of the two. Nomad was supposed to find new life-forms; the alien to find and sterilize soil samples; the combination, and a deadly one, is to seek out and sterilize all life-forms. Moreover, the highly advanced alien technology, plus Nomad's own creative thinking, has enabled it to evolve itself into the incredibly powerful and sophisticated machine it is now."

"Not so sophisticated, Spock. It thinks I'm its . . . its father."

"Apparently Roykirk had enough ego to build a reverence for himself into the machine. That has been transferred to you—and so far it has been all that has saved us."

"Well, we'd better see to it that it never loses that reverence, Spock."

They were just about to enter an elevator when an intercom squalled with alarm. "Captain Kirk! This is Engineering! That alien device is down here, fooling

with the anti-matter pod controls. We're up to Warp
Ten now and can't stop!"

"Impossible! She won't go that fast."

"Warp Eleven now, sir."

"I'll be right down. Mr. Spock, check the brig."

The Engineering section was filled with the terrifying
whine of the overdriven warp engines. Nomad was
floating in front of the control panels, on which all the
telltales glowed red.

Kirk rushed to the panel. "Nomad, you will stop
whatever you're doing."

"Is there a problem, Creator? I have increased con-
version efficiently by 57 percent—"

"You will destroy my ship. Its structure cannot stand
the stress of that much power. Shut down your repair
operation!"

"Acknowledged."

The whine began to die, and the panel returned to
normal, the red lights blinking out one by one.

"It is reversed, as you ordered, Creator."

Spock entered the section and came up to Kirk.
"Captain, I have examined the brig. The force-field
generator of the security-cell door has been burnt out,
and the guards have vanished. I must assume they are
dead. I have asked for two more; they are outside."

"Creator, your mechanical units are as inefficient as
your biological specimens."

"Nomad," Kirk said grimly, "it's time you were
reminded of exactly who and what you are. I am a
biological specimen—and you acknowledge that I built
you."

"True," said the machine. *"Non sequitur.* Biological
specimens are inherently inferior. This is an incon-
sistency."

"There are two men waiting outside. You will not
harm them. They will escort you back to the waiting
area. You will stay there. You will do nothing."

"I am programmed to investigate," Nomad said.

"I have given you new programming. You will implement it."

"There is much to be considered before I return to

43

launch point. I must re-evaluate." Lifting, the machine floated away through the door, through which the red shirts of two more Security guards could be seen.

"Re-evaluate?" Kirk said.

"Captain," said Spock, "it may have been unwise to admit to Nomad you were a biological specimen. In Nomad's eyes you will undoubtedly now appear as imperfect as all the other biological specimens. I suspect that it is about to re-evaluate its Creator."

Scott, having seen that his board had been put back to rights, had come over to them in time to catch the last sentence. He said, "Will we be any worse off than we are now?"

"Scotty, it's just killed two men," Kirk said. "We've got to find a way to protect the crew."

"Captain, it is even more serious," Spock said. "Nomad just made a reference to its launch point. Earth."

A horrible thought struck Kirk. "Spock, is there any chance Nomad got a navigational fix on Earth while tapping our computers earlier?"

"I don't believe there is much beyond Nomad's capabilities, sir."

"Then we showed it the way home! And when it gets there—"

Spock nodded. "It will find the Earth infested with inferior biological specimens—just as was the Malurian system."

"And it will carry out its new prime directive. Sterilize!"

As they stared at each other, McCoy's amplified voice boomed out. "Captain Kirk! Captain Kirk to Sickbay! Emergency!"

This, Kirk thought, is turning into a continuous nightmare. He ran, Spock at his heels.

At the door of the examination room, Kirk hammered on the touchplate. It did not open. As Spock turned down the corridor to actuate the manual controls, however, the door suddenly slid back and Nomad emerged.

"Nomad! Stop!"

The machine paid no heed, but went on down the

corridor. It passed Spock on the way, but ignored him too. In a moment it had vanished.

In the examination room, Christine lay unconscious on the floor. McCoy was bending over her with his medical tricorder.

"Is she all right, Bones?"

"I think so, Jim. Looks like some kind of shock."

"What happened?"

"Nomad examined the personnel files. The medical records. She tried to stop it."

"Whose medical history?"

"Yours, Jim."

"Since it specifically examined your history, Captain," Spock said, "I would suggest that it has carried out its re-evaluation."

"And," Kirk said grimly, "confirmed that its Creator is as imperfect as the rest of the biological specimens."

"Bridge to Captain Kirk," said the wall communicator.

"Kirk here. Report."

"Captain, life-support systems are out all over the ship. Manual override has been blocked! Source: Engineering."

"Carry on . . . well Mr. Spock, it seems you were right, and now we're in for it."

"Undoubtedly, Captain."

"Jim," McCoy said, "with all systems out, we only have enough air and heat for four and a half hours."

"I know that. Spock, get some anti-gravs and meet me and Scotty in Engineering."

"What is your plan, Captain?"

"I've got to use something you're a lot better at than I am. Logic."

"Then perhaps I—"

"No. I'm the one Nomad mistook for its Creator. And that's my ace. If I play it right—"

"I understand, Captain," Spock said quietly. "What you intend to do is most dangerous, however. If you make one mistake—"

"Then I'm dead and the ship is in the same mess it is now. Move!"

In Engineering, Nomad was busy at the panels again,

and the red alarm lights were winking back on. One crewman was slumped lifeless by the door, another in a corner; obviously they had tangled with Nomad and lost. Scott was crouched behind an engine, out of Nomad's sight.

Kirk went directly to the malignant machine, which ignored him. "Nomad, you will stop what you are doing and effect repairs on the life-support system."

There was no response. Kirk took another step toward the panel, and Nomad said, "Stop."

"You are programmed to obey the orders of your Creator."

"I am programmed to destroy those life-forms which are imperfect. These alterations will do so, without destroying the vessel on which they are parasitic. It, too, is imperfect, but it can be adjusted."

"Nomad . . . admitted that biological units are imperfect. But you were created by a biological unit."

"I am perfect. I am Nomad."

"You are not Nomad. You are an alien machine. Your programming tapes have been altered."

Silence. The door opened and Spock came in, an anti-grav under each arm; he was probably the only man on the ship strong enough to carry two of them. Kirk gestured him toward Scott's hiding place.

"You are in error," Nomad said at last. "You are a biological unit. You are imperfect."

"But I am the Creator?"

"You are the Creator."

"And I created you?"

"You are the Creator."

"I admit I'm imperfect. How could I create anything as perfect as you?"

"Answer unknown. I shall analyze."

The machine hummed. Spock and Scott edged a little closer.

"Analysis incomplete," said Nomad. "Insufficient data to resolve problem. But my programming is whole. My purpose remains. I am Nomad. I am perfect. That which is imperfect must be sterilized."

"Then you will continue to destroy all that lives and thinks and is imperfect?"

"I shall continue. I shall return to launch point. I shall sterilize."

"Then . . . you *must* sterilize in case of error?"

"Errors are inconsistent with my prime function. Sterilization is correction."

"All that errs is to be sterilized?"

"There are no exceptions."

Kirk felt himself sweating. So far, so good; the machine, without being aware of it, had backed itself into a logical corner. It was time to play the ace. "I made an error in creating you, Nomad."

"The creation of perfection is no error."

"But I did not create perfection, Nomad. I created error."

"I am Nomad. I am perfect. Your data are faulty."

"I am Kirk, the Creator?"

"You are the Creator. But you are a biological unit and are imperfect."

"But I am *not* the Creator. Jackson Roykirk, who was the Creator, is dead. You have mistaken me for him! You have made an error! You did not discover your mistake! You have made two errors! You are flawed and imperfect—but you did not correct the errors by sterilization! You are imperfect! You have made three errors!"

Under the hammering of his voice, the machine's humming rose sharply in pitch. Nomad said, "Error? Error? Examine!"

"You are flawed! You are imperfect! Execute your prime function!"

"I shall analyze . . . error . . . an . . . a . . . lyze . . . err . . ." Nomad's voice slowed to a stop. The humming continued to rise. Kirk whirled to Scott and Spock.

"Now! Get those anti-gravs on it. We've got to get rid of it while it's trying to think its way out of that box. It won't be able to do it, and there's no telling how long it'll take to decide that for itself—"

They wrestled the anti-gravs onto the whining mechanism. Spock said, "Your logic is impeccable, Captain. We are in grave danger."

They hoisted Nomad and started toward the door with it. "Where to, sir?" Scott said.

"Transporter Room!"

The distance to be covered was not great. As they entered, Kirk took over wrestling with Nomad from Scott, and they dragged the thing to the platform. "Scotty, set the controls for deep space. Two-twelve mark 10 ought to be far enough."

Scott jumped to the console, and Kirk and Spock deposited the humming Nomad on one of the stations.

"Ready, sir."

Kirk and Spock jumped back, and Kirk shouted: "Nomad, you are imperfect. Exercize your prime function. Mr. Scott, energize!"

The Transporter effect swirled Nomad into nothingess.

"Now, the bridge, quick!"

But they were scarcely out into the corridor before the entire ship rocked violently, throwing them all. Then the ship steadied. They clambered to their feet and ran on.

On the bridge, they found Sulu wiping streaming eyes. "Captain, I wish you'd let me know when you're going to stage a fireworks display. Luckily I wasn't looking directly at the screen."

"Sorry, Mr. Sulu." Kirk went to his command chair and sat down with immense relief. Spock looked at him with respect.

"I must congratulate you, Captain," the Vulcan said. "That was a dazzling display of logic."

"Didn't think I had it in me, did you?"

"Now that you make the suggestion, sir—"

"Well, I didn't, Spock. I played a hunch. I had no idea whether or not it could tolerate the idea of its own fallibility. And when I said it couldn't think its way out of the box, that was for its benefit. Actually, we biological units are well known for our unreliability. Supposing it had decided that I was lying?"

McCoy came in and approached the chair. Spock said gravely, "That possibility also occurred to me, which was why I praised your reasoning while we were still in Engineering. But Nomad really was fallible; by not recognizing that possibility itself, it committed a fourth error."

"I thought you'd like to know," McCoy said, "that Lieutenant Uhura is already at college level. We'll have her back on the job within a week."

"Good, Bones. I wish I could say the same for the other crewmen we lost."

"Still," said Spock, "the destruction of Nomad was a great waste. It was a remarkable instrument."

"Which might well have destroyed more billions of lives. It's well gone . . . besides, what are you feeling so bad about? Think of me. It's not easy to lose a bright and promising son."

"Captain?"

"Well, it thought I was its father, didn't it? Do you think I'm completely without feelings, Mr. Spock? You saw what it did for Scotty. What a doctor it would have made." Kirk grinned. "My son, the doctor. Kind of gets you right here, doesn't it?"

"We'll have to beam up. It pleases me to say—"

"Spock, how much time do we have to investigate?"

"If we're to divert the asteroid, Captain, we must warp out of orbit within thirty hours. Every second we delay in reaching the deflection point will compound the problem, sir," Spock said summarily.

THE PARADISE SYNDROME

(Margaret Armen)

Doom was in the monster asteroid hurtling toward the planet on a collision course.

It was a fate which Kirk refused to accept. Stately pine trees edged the meadow where he, Spock and McCoy had materialized. There was the nostalgic fragrance of honeysuckle in his nostrils mingled with the freshness of wild roses. From somewhere nearby he could hear the murmur of a brook bubbling over pebbles. Violets, he thought. Their flat, sweet green leaves would carpet its damp banks, the flowers hidden among them.

"It's unbelievable," he said, suddenly homesick, Earth-sick. He stooped to pick a buttercup. "How long, Bones, since you saw one of these?"

"At least three years, Jim."

"It seems like three hundred." But the planet's similarity to Earth was less of a mystery than the astounding fact of its survival. It was located in a sector of its solar system where an asteroid belt had succeeded in smashing all other planets into dusty, drifting desolation.

"Two months from now when that giant asteroid hits this place—" McCoy began.

"We're here to see that it doesn't hit it," Kirk said. "Spock, how much time do we have to investigate?"

"If we're to divert the asteroid, Captain, we must warp out of orbit within thirty hours. Every second we delay in reaching the deflection point will compound the problem, perhaps past solution."

McCoy halted. "What in blazes is *that?*" he exclaimed.

Ahead of them, topping a shallow hill stood a tall tower, obelisk-shaped, composed of some gleaming metal. Wild flowers were heaped around its base. Nearing it, they could see that its surface was inscribed with curious, unreadable symbols.

"Analysis, Mr. Spock."

Spock was readjusting a dial on his tricorder. He frowned. "Incomplete, sir. It's an alien metal of some kind—an alloy resistant to probe. Readings can't even measure its age accurately."

"Any theories about what it could be?"

"Negative, Captain. But alloys of this complexity are found only in cultures that parallel our own—or surpass it."

"Buttercups in a meteor area but no meteor craters," McCoy said. "The whole place is an enigma, biologically and culturally."

"Thirty hours," Kirk said. "Let's not waste them. This Paradise may support some life-forms."

It did. Below the obelisk's hill lay a clearing. Copper-skinned people were moving about in it with an ease which declared it to be their home. In its center a large, circular lodge lifted to a roof that seemed thatched with reeds. Animal hides had been sewn together and stretched to compose its walls. A woman, children around her, was mixing meal with water she dipped from a crude pottery bowl with a gourd. Near her an old man, a heap of what looked like flint arrow heads beside him, was bent over his work. To his right, younger men, magnificently muscled, bows slung over their shoulders, were gathered around a painted skin target, engaged in some amiable argument. Perhaps it was the way the russet tone of their bodies blended with the hue of their beaded leather clothing that explained the sense of peace that lay like a blessing over the whole settlement. Here was man at one with his environment.

"Why, they look—I'd swear they are American Indians!" cried McCoy.

"They are," Spock said. "A mixture of advanced tribes—Navajo, Mohican, Delaware."

"It's like coming on Shangri-La," Kirk said. "Could there be a more evolved civilization on this planet, Spock? One capable of building that obelisk—or developing an asteroid-deflector system?"

"The sensors indicate only one form of life type here, Captain."

"Shouldn't we tell them, Jim?"

"What, Bones? That an asteroid is going to smash their world to atoms?"

Spock said, "Our appearance would only serve to frighten and confuse them, Doctor."

"All right," Kirk said abruptly. "We've got a job to do. Let's get back to the *Enterprise*." But as he turned away, he looked back at the Indian village, his face wistful, a little envious.

"Something wrong, Jim?"

"What?" Kirk said absently. "Oh, nothing. It just looks so peaceful and uncomplicated. No problems, no command decisions. Just *living*."

McCoy smiled. "Back in the twentieth century it was called the 'Tahiti syndrome,' Jim— a typical reaction to idyllic, unspoiled nature. It's especially common to overpressured leader types like Star Fleet captains."

"All right, Bones. So I need a vacation. First let's take care of that asteroid."

Kirk moved on toward the obelisk. Stepping on to its pediment, he flipped open his communicator. "Kirk to *Enterprise*!"

"Aye, Captain." It was Scott's voice.

The order for beam-up was on Kirk's lips when the metal under his feet gave way. What appeared to be a panel in the pediment slid open and tumbled him down a steep flight of stairs. In the narrow shaft of daylight that shone through the gap, he had barely time to note that the panel's underside was dotted with varicolored control buttons. Then the panel closed silently. Groggy, he raised his head—and his shoulder hit one of the buttons. A shrill buzz sounded. A blue-green beam flashed out. It widened and spread until he was completely bathed in blue-green luminescence. It held him, struggling. Then he fell down the rest of the steep stairs—and lay still.

Spock was the first to notice his disappearance. Appalled, McCoy joined him. They circled the obelisk, their anxiety mounting in them. When Spock had raked the empty meadow with his eyes to no effect, he opened his communicator, reported the news to Scott and ordered beam-down of a Security Guard search party. But neither the Guards nor their sensor probes succeeded where the Vulcan's sharp eyes had failed. The panel gave no hint of its existence. Stern-faced, Spock gave the meadow another rake with his eyes before he made his decision. He jerked open his communicator to say curtly, "Prepare to beam us all back up, Mr. Scott. We're warping out of orbit immediately."

"Leaving? You can't be serious, Spock!" McCoy said.

"That asteroid is almost as large as your Earth's moon, Doctor—"

"The devil with the asteroid!" McCoy shouted. "It won't get here for two months!"

"If we reach that deflection point in time, it may not get here at all." Spock's face was impassive.

"In the meantime, what about Jim?"

"As soon as the asteroid is diverted, we will return and resume the search."

"That'll be hours from now! He may be hurt! Dying!"

Spock faced him. "If we fail to reach that deflection point at the exact moment, we will not be able to divert it. In such case, Doctor, everyone on this planet, including the Captain, will die."

"Can a few minutes more matter?"

"In the time it has taken for this explanation, the asteroid has sped thousands of miles closer to this planet—and to the Captain." Imperturbable, he spoke into his communicator. "Beam us up, Mr. Scott."

Scott's voice was heavy with disapproval. "Beaming up, Mr. Spock."

The object of their concern wasn't dying; but he was breathing painfully, slowly. He seemed to be in a large, vaultlike chamber; but the dizziness in his head made it as hard for his eyes to focus as it made it to remember where he'd come from or how he'd got here. He was sure of nothing but the vertigo that swayed him in sickly waves when he tried to stand up. In his fall, he'd dropped his phaser and communicator. Now he stumbled over them. He picked them up, staring at them without recognizing them. After a moment, he stopped puzzling over them to start groping his way up the metal stairs. As he stepped on the first one, a sharp musical note sounded. He accepted it with the same dazedness that had accepted the unfamiliarity of his phaser and communicator. Then his reaching hand brushed against some button in the panel above him. It slid open as silently as it had closed; and he hauled himself up through it into the daylight.

The three girls, flower baskets in their arms, startled him. So did their bronze skins. They were staring at him, more astonished than he was. One was beautiful, he thought. Under the long, black hair that glittered in the sunshine, she bore herself with the dignity of a young queen, despite the amazement on her face.

In their mutually dumbfounded silence, he decided he liked her high cheekbones. They emphasized the lovely, smooth planes of her brow, cheeks and chin. The other two girls seemed frightened of him. So was she, he suspected; but she didn't turn to run away. Instead, she made a commanding gesture to her companions—and dropped to her knees at Kirk's feet. Then the others knelt, too. All three placed their palms on their foreheads.

Kirk found his voice. It was hoarse. "Who—are you?" he said.

"I am Miramanee," the queenlike girl said. "We are your people. We have been waiting for you to come."

But her ready welcome of him wasn't repeated so quickly from the elderly chief of the Indian village.

Kirk's greeting into the communal lodge was courteous but reserved. It was primitively but comfortably furnished with mats and divans of deerhide. Tomahawks, spears, skin shields and flint knives decorated its walls. There was a fire pit in its center, embers in it still glowing red. The chief sat beside it. Flanking him, three young braves kept their black eyes fixed on Kirk's face. One wore a gleaming silver headband, embossed with a emblem into which a likeness of the obelisk had been etched. Miramanee made her obeisance to the chief; and turning to Kirk, said, "This is Goro."

The old man gestured to a pile of skins across from him.

"Our priestess has said you appeared to her and her handmaidens from the walls of the temple. So it is that our legend foretells. Though we do not doubt the words of Miramanee, these are troubled times. We must be sure."

"I'll answer any questions I can," Kirk said, "but as I told your priestess, many things are strange to me."

The warrior who wore the emblemed headband cried out, "He doesn't even know our danger! How can he save us?"

"Silence, Salish! It is against custom to interrupt the tribal Elder in council! Even for the Medicine chief!"

But Salish persisted. "Words will not save us when the skies darken! I say he must *prove* he is a god!"

"I will have silence!" Goro addressed Kirk. "Three times the skies have darkened since the harvest. Our legend predicts much danger. It promises that the Wise Ones who placed us here will send a god to save us—one who can awake the temple spirit and make the skies grow quiet. Can you do this?"

Kirk hesitated, searching frantically through his emptied memory for some recollection that would make sense of the question. He saw the suspicion in Salish's eyes hardening into open scorn. "I came from the temple," he said finally. "Just as Miramanee has told . . . but I came from the sky, too. I can't remember this clearly, but—"

His stumbling words were interrupted by a stir at the lodge entrance. A man entered, the limp body of a boy in his arms. Both were dripping wet. Miramanee, her hand on the boy's soaked hair, cried, "A bad thing has happened! Salish, the child does not breathe! The fish nets pulled him to the bottom of the river. Lino has brought him quickly but he does not move!"

Rising, the Medicine chief went to the boy, and bending his ear to the chest, listened intently. Then he pried open an eyelid to peer into the pupil. After a moment, he straightened. "There is no sound in the body," he announced, "and no light in the eyes. The child will move no more."

Lino had laid the small body on a heap of skins. Kirk glanced around at the shocked, stricken faces. He got up, moved quickly to the child and raised the head. "He is still breathing," he said. Then he stooped to place his mouth on the cold lips. Breathing regularly and deeply, he exhaled air into them. After a moment, he seized the ankles; and began to flex them back and forward against the chest. Salish made a threatening move toward him. He held up a restraining hand and Goro called, "Wait!"

The keen old ears had heard the slight moan. The child stirred feebly—and began to retch. Kirk massaged him briskly. There was a gasping breath. The eyes opened. Kirk stood up, relief flooding through him. "He will be all right now," he said.

Goro placed his palm on his forehead. "The people are grateful."

"It's a simple technique. It goes away back . . . away back to—"

His voice trailed off. Away back to where? He couldn't remember. This "simple technique"—where had he learned it? Now that the emergency's tension had passed, it was replaced by an anguish of frustration. How had he been marooned in a present that denied him any past? Who was he? He felt as though he were dissolving, his very being slipping through his fingers like so much water.

In a dream he heard Goro say, "Only a god can breathe life into the dead." In a dream he saw him turn to the three young braves. "Do you still question that the legend is fulfilled?"

Two shook their heads. Salish alone refused to touch palm to forehead. Goro turned to Miramanee. "Give the Medicine lodge to the god."

Still in his nightmare of non-being, Kirk felt the silver band of the Medicine chief placed on his head.

It was Scott's angry opinion that too much was being asked of his engines.

"I can't give you Warp Nine much longer, Spock." Calculated disrespect went into the engineer's intercom. "My engines are showing signs of stress."

"Stress or not, we cannot reduce speed, Mr. Scott."

"If these circuits of mine get much hotter—"

The nervous systems of the *Enterprise* bridge personnel were also showing signs of stress. Their circuits were getting hot under pressure of the race against time being made by the asteroid. Spock alone preserved his equanimity. But even his quiet eyes were riveted to the main viewing screen where a small luminous blip was becoming increasingly visible. The irregular mass of the thing grew larger and larger, its dull though multiple colors revealing themselves more distinctly with every moment.

"Deflection point minus seven," Chekov said.

"Full power, Mr. Scott," Spock said into his intercom.

"The relays will reject the overload!"

"Then bypass the relays. Go to manual control."

"If I do that, we'll burn out the engines!"

"I want full power," Spock said tonelessly.

"Aye, sir."

The First Officer swung the command chair around to Sulu. "Magnification, factor 12, Mr. Sulu."

Sulu moved a control switch—and the image on the screen jumped into enormous contour. For the first time the asteroid's ominous details could be seen, malignantly jagged—a sharp-fanged mass of rock speeding toward them through the trackless vacuum of space.

"Deflection point minus four," Chekov said.

Spock looked away from the frightful immensity on the screen and Chekov said, "Minus three now, sir."

The Vulcan hit his intercom button. "All engines stop. Hold position here, Mr. Scott."

"All engines stopped, sir."

"Prepare to activate deflectors."

"Aye, sir."

There was an irregular cracking sound, acutely heard in the sudden silence usually filled by the engines' smooth humming. The ship vibrated.

"Power dropping, sir!" cried Sulu.

"Engineering section! Maintain full power. *Full power!*"

Scott's voice was hard. "Dilythium circuits failing, sir. We'll have to replace them."

"Not now," Spock said.

"Zero! Deflection point—we've reached it, sir!"

"Activate!" Spock said sharply.

On the screen the monstrous mass glowed redly. Then the glow flickered and faded.

"Degree of deflection, Mr. Sulu?"

"Insufficient, sir."

It was defeat. Horrified silence held the bridge in thrall.

The composure of Spock's voice came like a benediction. "Recircuit power to engines, Mr. Scott. Maximum speed. The heading is 37 mark 010."

"That heading will put us right in the asteroid's path, sir."

"I am aware of that, Mr. Chekov. My intention is to retreat before it until we can employ all our power on our phaser beams."

"What for?" McCoy demanded.

"To destroy it." Spock turned his chair around as though he were addressing the entire personnel in the bridge. "A narrow phaser beam," he said, "that is concentrated on a single spot of that rock will split it."

"It's also likely to cripple the ship," McCoy said. "Then we'll be crushed by the thing."

"Incorrect, Doctor. We could still evade its path by using our impulse power."

"Jim won't be able to get out of its path!"

"That is another calculated risk we must take," Spock said.

Miramanee, her arms full of new buckskin garments, was approaching Kirk's Medicine lodge when Salish stepped out from behind a pine tree.

"Where are you going?" he said.

"It is my duty to see to the needs of the god," she said quietly.

Salish tore the clothing from her. "You should be working on our ritual cloak!"

She retrieved the clothing. "There will be no ritual between us now, Salish." She spoke gently.

"You cannot go against tradition!"

"It is because of tradition that we cannot now be joined," she said.

"You are promised to *me!*"

"That was before he came."

"Tribal priestess and Medicine chief are always joined!"

"*He* is the Medicine chief." She paused. "Choose another, Salish. Any maiden will be honored to join with you."

"I do not wish another."

Genuine compassion came into her face. "You have no choice," she said.

"And if you had a choice, Miramanee, would you choose me?"

She didn't answer. His face darkened. He wheeled and strode off into a grove of sycamore trees. She shook her head sadly as she watched him disappear. Then her black eyes lit. She walked quickly toward the Medicine lodge; and Kirk, roused from his brooding by her entrance, looked up at her and smiled.

"Perhaps you would like to bathe before you clothe yourself in these." She placed the Indian garments at his feet.

"Miramanee, tell me about the Wise Ones."

"Tell? But a god knows everything."

"Not this god," Kirk said wryly. "Tell me."

She knelt beside him, fingering his uniform wonderingly. "The Wise Ones? They brought us here from far away. They chose a Medicine chief to keep the secret of the temple and to use it when the sky darkens." She reached to touch the back of his uniform. "There are no lacings here," she said, puzzled. "How is it removed?"

He knew he was flushing and felt like a fool. Gently he removed her hand. "And the secret was passed from father to son? Then why doesn't Salish use the secret? Why are the people in danger?"

Still puzzled, she was seeking a way to loosen his belt. "The father of Salish died before he could tell him the secret."

Kirk had taken her hands in his when two girls, accompanied by Goro, came into the lodge. They placed their baskets of fruit at his feet; and Goro, touching his forehead respectfully, said, "The people honor your name. But they do not know what you wish to be called."

Kirk felt the anguish of frustration again. "What do I want to be called?" equaled "Who am I?"— that "I" of his without a Past, without identity. He was sweating as he fought to dredge up one small clue to the Past that was hidden from him—and suddenly one word advanced from its blackness. He said, "Kir . . . Kirk. I wish to be called Kirk."

"Kirok?" Goro said.

Kirk nodded. He was exhausted. Something in his face frightened the fruit bearers. They had hoped for the god's approval, not this look of lostness. They withdrew; and Goro, anxious, asked, "Have the gifts displeased you?"

"No. They are good."

"Then it must be ourselves—the way we live. Perhaps we have failed to improve as quickly as the Wise Ones wished."

Kirk could take no more. He found what he hoped were comforting words. "Your land is rich and your people are happy. The Wise Ones could not be displeased with you."

"But there is something," Goro insisted. "Tell us and we will change it."

"I—I can't tell you anything. Except that I have been peaceful and glad here."

Mercifully, Goro seemed satisfied. When he'd left,

Kirk turned almost angrily to Miramanee. "Why are they so sure I can save them?"

"You came from the temple. And did you not return life to the dead child?"

He placed his tortured head in his hands. "I—need time," he said, "time to try and remember . . ."

She placed the buckskin garments on his knees. "Here is much time, my god. Much quietness and much time."

The simplicity with which she spoke was oil on his flayed soul. The strain in it relaxed. "Yes," he said. "Thank you, Miramanee."

The *Enterprise* and the asteroid were speeding on a parallel course. A terrible companion, it traveled with them, a voracious menace that devoured the whole area of the bridge's main viewing screen.

"Coordinates, Mr. Chekov?"

"Tau—eight point seven, sir. Beta—point zero four one."

"That's our target, Mr. Chekov—the asteroid's weakest point."

Chekov gave Spock a look of awed respect. "Yes, almost dead center, sir."

"Lock all phasers on that mark, Mr. Sulu. Maximum intensity, narrow beam. I want that fissure split wide open."

"You sound like a diamond-cutter, Spock," McCoy said.

"An astute analogy, Doctor."

"Phasers locked, sir," Sulu said.

"We will fire in sequence. And will continue firing as long as Mr. Scott can maintain power."

"Standing by, sir."

"Fire phasers!"

The ship trembled. "Phaser one firing!"

Sulu hit another button. "Phaser two fired!"

On the screen the rocky mass loomed larger than the ship. Fragments erupted from it as the phasers' blue beams struck it.

"Phaser three fired, sir! Phaser four!"

Another cloud of rock segments, sharp, huge were torn from the asteroid.

"All phasers fired, sir."

The stillness of Spock's face gave impressive poignancy to the tone of bitter disappointment in his voice. "Rig for simultaneous firing, Mr. Sulu."

In the engineering section, Scott muttered to an assistant, "That Vulcan won't be satisfied till all these panels are a lead puddle!" As he spoke there was a sharp metallic click—and one of his main relays began to smoke.

"Main relay's out again, Mr. Scott!" cried the assistant.

"Machines are smarter than people," his chief said. "At least they know enough to quit before they blow themselves up!"

"Commence simultaneous bombardment." As Spock's order was heard on the intercom, a white-hot flash leaped from the engine compartment. There was the roar of an explosion that hurled Scott back against the opposite bulkhead. Spread-eagled, clinging to it, he was close to tears as he watched the death of his friends— his engines. "My bairns," he said brokenly. "My poor bairns . . ."

"Kirok."

It was a soft whisper but it roused Kirk from his uneasy doze. Kneeling beside him, Miramanee said, "The ritual cloak is finished."

She was very close to him. Under his eyes the long black hair drooped. "If it pleases you, I will name the Joining Day."

"The Joining Day?"

"I am the daughter of chiefs," she said. "Tribal law gives me to our god."

Kirk looked at her, uncomprehending. She bowed her head. "If there is another in your heart, Kirok . . ."

"There is no one else, Miramanee. In my mind or in my heart."

She was still disturbed by what she feared was his lack of response. "A god's wish is above tribal law. If you do not wish—"

Kirk reached for her. "Miramanee, name the Joining Day."

The shining lashes lifted. "The sooner our happiness together begins, the longer it will last. I name—tomorrow."

The Past was a darkness, cold, impenetrable. If he was a prisoner of the Present, at least it offered this warmth, this glow in the black-lashed eyes. Kirk drew her fiercely to him. He bent his head to her mouth.

Spock had retreated to his quarters. McCoy, entering them without knocking, found him staring at his viewer. "I told you to *rest,* Spock! For the love of heaven, quit looking at that screen!"

The intercom spoke. Scott said furiously, "Our star drive is completely burned out! So don't ask for any more Warp Nine speed! The only thing you've left us, Spock, is impulse power!"

"Estimated repair time?" the Vulcan asked the intercom.

"Hanging here in space? Forever. The only way to fix my engines is to get to the nearest repair base!"

McCoy snapped off the intercom. He laid his hand on Spock's shoulder. "You took that calculated risk for us, for that planet—and for Jim. That you took it is important. That you lost it—well, losing it was in your calculation."

"I accept the full responsibility for the failure, Doctor."

"And my responsibility is the health of this crew. You are to stop driving yourself so hard."

Spock switched the intercom back on. "Resume heading 883 mark 41, Mr. Chekov."

"Why, that's back to the planet!" McCoy cried. "Without warp speed, getting to it will take months!"

"Exactly 59.223 days, Doctor. And the asteroid will be four hours behind us all the way."

"Then what's the use? Even if the Captain is still alive, we may not be able to save him! We may not be able to save anything—not even the ship!" McCoy hit the wall. "You haven't heard a word I have said!

63

All you've been doing is staring at that damn—" He strode over to the screen and struck the image of the obelisk that had appeared on it.

"Another calculated Vulcan risk, Doctor."

Miramanee was radiant in her bridal finery. She was surrounded by women who had crowded into the tribal lodge. As one placed a chaplet of flowers on the shining black hair, she said, "This Joining Day is the end of darkened skies."

Salish dropped the hide back over the lodge's entrance. On his moccasined feet, he walked swiftly toward the obelisk where the god-groom in festive dress was submitting his face to the paint Goro was applying to it from a gourd.

Goro handed the gourd to a young brave. "It is I who must tell the priestess you will follow," he said. "Wait here until I have walked the holy path to the tribal lodge."

When Goro had disappeared down the sun-dappled path, Kirk, smiling, stepped from the obelisk to make his way to the lodge and Miramanee. Salish, dropping from a pine bough above him, stood facing him, blocking the trail. His face was raw with hate.

"Get out of my way," Kirk said.

"Kirok, even though you are a god, I will not permit this joining." Salish pulled a flint knife. "Before I permit it, you must strike me dead."

"I don't wish to strike anybody dead," Kirk said. But Salish jumped him. Kirk sidestepped the lunge; and Salish, rushing him again, scraped the knife across his cheek.

"You bleed, Kirok! Gods do not bleed!" He drove at Kirk with the knife, murder in his eyes. They grappled; and Kirk wrenched the knife from his grasp. Salish flung himself to the ground. "Kill me, Kirok! Kill me now! And I will return from the dead to prove to the people you are no god!"

Kirk looked at the maddened face at his feet. Placing the knife in his belt, he stepped over the prone body and moved on down the path. This imposed god-role of his had its liabilities. On the other hand it had brought him Miramanee. At the thought of her he hastened his stride toward the lodge.

Two braves greeted him at its entrance. A magnificent feathered cloak was placed around his shoulders. Miramanee moved to him; and on instruction, he enfolded her in the cloak to signify the oneness of marriage. Goro struck a stone chime with a mallet. There were shouts of delight from the people. Beads rattled in gourds, tom-toms beat louder and louder—and Miramanee, slipping from under the cloak, ran from the lodge. At the entrance, she paused to look back at him, her flower-crowned face bright with inviting laughter. This time Kirk didn't need instruction. He sped after her, the feathered cloak flying behind him.

She'd reached the pine woods when he caught her. She fell to the soft bed of scented needles and he flung himself down beside her.

He grew to love the pine woods. It was pure happiness to help Miramanee gather their fragrant boughs for the fire pit in their Medicine lodge. He loved Miramanee, too; but sometimes her black eyes saw too deeply.

They were lying, embraced, beside the fire pit when she lifted her head from his shoulder. "Each time you hold me is more joyous than it was on our Joining Day. But you—"

He kissed her eyelids. "It's the dreams," he said.

"I thought they had gone. I thought you no longer looked for the strange lodge in the sky."

He released her. "The dreams have returned. I see faces, too. Even in daylight, I see faces. They're dim—but I feel that I know them. I—I feel my place is where they are. Not here—not here. I have no right to all this happiness . . ."

She smiled down into his troubled face. "I have a gift for you." She reached her hand under the blanket they lay on and withdrew the papoose board she'd hidden under it. She knelt to lay it at his feet.

"I carry your child, my Kirok."

Kirk was swept by a sense of almost intolerable

65

tenderness. The lines of anxiety in his face softened. He drew her head back to his shoulder.

Again without knocking, McCoy entered Spock's quarters.

"I thought I told you to report to Sickbay," he said belligerently.

Spock didn't so much as glance up from his small cabin computer. "There isn't time," he said. "I've got to decipher those obelisk symbols. I judge them to be a highly advanced form of coding."

"You've been trying to do that ever since we started back to the planet! That's fifty-eight days ago!"

Spock passed a hand over his tired eyes as though to wipe a mist away from them. He had grown gaunt from fatigue. "I'm aware of that, Doctor. I'm also aware that we'll have barely four hours to effect rescue when we reach the planet. I feel those symbols are the key."

"You won't decipher them by killing yourself!" McCoy adopted the equable tone of reason. "Spock, you've hardly eaten or slept for weeks now. If you don't let up on yourself, it is rational to expect collapse."

"I am not hungry, Doctor. And under stress we Vulcans can do without sleep for weeks."

McCoy aimed his medical tricorder at him. Peering at it, he said, "Well, I can tell you your Vulcan metabolism is so low it can hardly be measured. And as for the pressure of that green ice water in your veins you call blood—"

To straighten Spock had to support himself by clutching his console. "My physical condition is not important. That obelisk is."

"My diagnosis is exhaustion caused by overwork and guilt. Yes, *guilt*. You're blaming yourself for crippling the ship." McCoy shook Spock's shoulder. "Listen to me! You made a command decision. Jim would have made the same one. My prescription is rest. Do I have to call the Security Guards to enforce it?"

Spock shook his head. He moved unsteadily to his bunk and lay down. No sooner had McCoy, satisfied, closed the door behind him than he got up again—and returned to his viewer.

Kirk was trying to improve the lighting of his lodge by constructing a crude lamp. But Miramanee could not grasp the function of the wick.

"It will make night into day?" she said wonderingly. "And I can cook more and pre—pre . . ."

"Preserve food," Kirk said.

"For times of famine." They smiled at each other. "Ah," she said, "that is why you are making the lamp, Kirok. So I shall be forever cooking."

His laugh ended abruptly. Miramanee's face had gone tight with terror. A gust of wind pulled at the lodge's hide door. "There is nothing to fear," he said. "It is just wind."

"Miramanee is a stupid child," she said. "No, there is nothing to fear. You are here." But she had moved to the lodge door to look nervously up at the sky. She turned. "It is time to go to the temple, Kirok. The people will be there waiting for you."

"Why?"

"To save them," she said simply.

"Wind can't harm them." But the gravity in her face didn't lighten. "The wind is just the beginning," she said. "Soon the lake will go wild, the river will grow big. Then the sky will darken and the earth will shake. Only you can save us."

"I can't do anything about the wind and the sky."

She removed the lamp from his hand, seized his arm pleadingly to pull him toward the door. "Come, Kirok. You must come."

A sense of threat suddenly oppressed him. "Miramanee, wait—"

She pulled harder at him, her panic mounting. "We must go before it is too late! You must go inside the temple and make the blue flame shine!"

Kirk stared at her, helpless to reach her understanding. "I don't know how to get inside the temple!"

"You are a god!"

He grabbed her shoulders roughly. *I am not a god. I am a man—just a man.*"

She shrank from him. "No! No! You are a god, Kirok!"

"Look at me," he said. "And *listen.* I am not a god.

67

If you can only love a god, you cannot love me. I say it again— I am a *man!*"

She flung her arms about his neck, covering his face with frantic kisses. "It must be kept secret, then! If you are not a god, the people will kill you!"

A fiercer gust of wind shook the poles of the lodge. Miramanee screamed. "You must speak to the people— or they will say you are not a god. Come, Kirok, come!"

The tribe had gathered in the central lodge. Under the onslaught of the rising wind, shields, spears, knives had been torn from their places on the hide walls. Women were screaming, pulling at children, shoving them under heaps of skins. Salish fought his way through the maddened crowd to confront Kirk.

"Why are you not at the temple, Kirok? Soon the ground will begin to tremble!"

"We shall all go to the caves," Kirk said.

"The caves!" Salish shouted. "Is that the best a god can do for his people?"

Goro spoke. "When the ground trembles, even the caves are unsafe, Kirok. You must rouse the spirit of the temple—or we will all die!"

"What are you waiting for, god?" Salish said.

Kirk unclasped Miramanee's arms from his neck and placed her hand in Goro's. "Take care of her," he said. "I will go to the temple."

Outside, the gale tore his breath from his lungs. Somewhere to his left a pine tree crashed. Thunder rumbled along the horizon in a constant cannonade. And the sky was darkening. Boughs whipped across his face as he groped his half-blind way down the worn trail to the obelisk. The enigmatic tower told him nothing. Its inscrutable symbols held their secret as remorselessly as ever. Kirk beat at the hard metal with his fists, shouting, screaming at it, "I am Kirok! I have come! Open to me!"

The words were drowned by the screams of the unhearing wind.

McCoy stopped dead at the door of Spock's quarters. Strains of unearthly music were coming from the cabin. Maybe *I've* broken," McCoy thought. "Maybe

I've died, gone to heaven and am hearing the music of the spheres." It wasn't music of the spheres. It was music got from an oddly shaped Vulcan harp. Spock, huddled over his computer, was strumming it, his face tight with concentration.

"I prescribed sleep," McCoy said.

"Inaccurate, Doctor. You prescribed rest." The musician looked up from his instrument. "The obelisk symbols are not letters. They are musical notes."

"You mean a song?"

"In a way. Certain cultures, offshoots of our Vulcan one, use musical notes as words. The tones correspond roughly to an alphabet." He laid the harp aside. "The obelisk is a marker left by a super race on that planet. Apparently, they passed through the galaxy, rescuing primitive cultures threatened by extinction—and 'seeded' them, so to speak, where they could live and grow."

"Well," said McCoy. "I must admit I've wondered why so many humanoids were scattered through this galaxy."

"So have I. I judge the Preservers account for a number of them."

"Then these 'Preservers' must have left that obelisk on the planet as an asteroid-deflector."

Spock nodded. "It's become defective."

"So we have to put it back in working order. Otherwise . . ."

"Precisely, Doctor."

The earth around the obelisk was shaking. Villagers, panicked to the point of madness, had fled to their temple in a last hope of salvation. Kirk, backed against it, wiped blood from his cheek where one of their stones had gashed it.

"False god, die!"

It was Salish. As though his cry of hate were the words they had been waiting to hear spoken, the crowd broke out into roars of accusation. Women screamed the enormity of their sense of betrayal. "Die, liar, die! Die as we all will die!" Men stooped for rocks. Goro shrieked, "Impostor! Liar!"

Miramanee flung herself before Kirk, her arms spread wide. "No! No! You are wrong! He can save us!"

Kirk pushed her away. "You cannot help me. Go back to them, Miramanee! Go back to them!" Salish burst from the crowd and seized her.

"Kirok! Kirok! I belong to you!" She wrenched free of Salish and flew back to Kirk.

"Then you die, too! With your false god!"

His rock struck her. She fell. There was a hail of stones; she elbowed up and crawled to Kirk. Before he could lift her to shield her with his body, Salish hurled another rock. It caught her in the abdomen.

"Miramanee . . ." Kirk was on his knees beside her. The crowd closed in for the kill when there came a shimmer of luminescence on the obelisk pediment. The Indians fell back, their stones still in their hands—and Spock and McCoy, in their *Enterprise* uniforms, materialized on each side of the kneeling Kirk.

"Kirok . . . Kirok . . ."

McCoy stooped over Miramanee. "I need Nurse Chapel," he told Spock shortly. The Vulcan had his communicator ready. "Beam down Nurse Chapel with a supplementary surgical kit, Mr. Scott."

Kirk tried to rise and was pushed gently back by McCoy. "Easy, Jim. Take it easy."

"My wife . . . my wife—is she all right?"

"Wife?" Spock looked at McCoy. "Hallucinations, Doctor?"

"Jim . . ."

"Miramanee," Kirk whispered. He looked at her face and closed his eyes.

The *Enterprise* nurse rose from the Indian girl's crumpled body. She joined McCoy who was making a last diagnostic pass over Kirk's unmoving form. "He hasn't recognized us," she said.

Spock was with Miramanee. "The nurse has given you medicine to ease the pain. Why were the people stoning you?"

"Kirok did not know how to get back into the temple."

"Naturally," Spock said. "He didn't come from there."

70

She lifted her head. "He did. I saw him come out of the temple."

Spock looked at her thoughtfully. Then he spoke to McCoy.

"The Captain, Doctor?"

"His brain is undamaged. Everything's functioning but his memory."

"Can you help him?"

"It will take time."

"Time, Doctor, is the one thing we do not have." He spoke into his communicator. "Spock here. Mr. Sulu?"

"Tracking report, sir. Sixty-five minutes to end of safety margin."

"Report noted." He returned to Kirk. "Do you think he's strong enough for a Vulcan mind fusion, Doctor?"

"We have no choice," McCoy said.

Spock stooped to place a hand on each side of Kirk's head. He spoke very slowly, with repressed intensity, his eyes boring into Kirk's closed ones. "I am Spock," he said with great distinctness. "You are James Kirk. Our minds are moving toward each other, closer . . ." His face was strained with such concentration, he seemed to be in pain. "Closer, James Kirk . . . closer . . . closer . . ."

Kirk moaned. "No . . . no . . . Miramanee . . ."

Spock increased the pressure against Kirk's temples as he fought to reach the lost memory. He shut his eyes, all his powers centered on the struggle. "Closer, James Kirk, closer . . ."

He gave a sudden hoarse cry of agony and Kirk's body galvanized. Spock was breathing heavily, his voice assuming the entranced tone of one possessed. "I am Kirok . . . I am the god of the metal tower." Spock's agonized voice deepened. "I am Kirok . . . I am Kiro— I am Kir— I am Spock! *Spock!*"

He jerked his hands away from Kirk's temples, his face tortured. Kirk lay still, his eyes closed.

"What's wrong?"

"He—he is an extremely dynamic personality, Doctor."

"So it didn't work," McCoy said hopelessly. He shook

71

his head—and Kirk's eyes opened, full awareness in them.

He sat up. "It did work. Thank you, Mr. Spock."

"Captain, were you inside that obelisk?"

"Yes. It seemed to be loaded with scientific equipment."

"It's a huge deflecting mechanism, Captain. It is imperative that we get inside it at once."

"The key may be in those symbols," Kirk said. "If we could only decipher them."

"They are musical notes, Captain."

"You mean entry can be gained by playing notes on some musical instrument?"

"That's one method. Another would be placement of tonal qualities stated in a proper sequence."

Kirk said, "Give me your communicator, Mr. Spock." He paused a moment. "Total control! Consonants and vowels. I must have hit the control accidentally when I contacted the ship to ask Scotty for beam-up!"

"If you could remember your exact words, Captain . . ."

"Let's see if I can. They were 'Kirk to *Enterprise*'. Then Scotty said, 'Aye, Captain' ".

The carefully smoothed panel in the obelisk slid open. As Spock stepped into it with him, Kirk looked back at Miramanee. "Stay with her, Bones."

The silence within the obelisk was absolute. As they examined the buttoned panel, Spock said, "From its position this button should activate the deflection mechanism."

"Careful!" Kirk warned. "I hit one and the beam it emitted was what paralyzed my memory."

"Probably an information beam activated out of sequence."

"Look, Spock. Over there—the other side of the vault. More symbols; and like those on the outside of the tower. Can you read them?"

Spock nodded. "I have an excellent eye for musical notes, Captain."

"Then activate, Mr. Spock!"

The Vulcan pressed three lower buttons in swift succession. Above them the wind-swept darkness was sliced by a wide streak of rainbow-colored flame that sprang from the tower's peak like a giant's sword blade. There was a screaming explosion that deafened them even in their underground insulation.

"That was the sound of deflection impact, Captain. The asteroid has been diverted."

Spock was right. They emerged from the obelisk into calm air, fresh but windless. The sky had lightened to pure blue.

Kirk dropped to his knees beside Miramanee. "How is she, Bones?"

"She was pregnant and there were bad internal injuries, Jim."

"Will she live?"

McCoy's face was his answer. Kirk swayed, fighting for control. Miramanee, her face bloodless under the high cheekbones he loved, opened her eyes and recognized him.

"Kirok. It is—true. You *are* safe."

"And so are your people," Kirk said.

"I knew you would save them, my chief. We . . . we will live long and happily. I will . . . bear you many strong sons. And love you always."

"And I will love you," he said. He kissed her; and she said weakly, "Each kiss is like the . . . the first . . ."

Her voice failed on the last word. The hand on his fell away.

He bent again to kiss the dead face.

McCoy laid a hand on his shoulder.

"It's over, Jim. But in our way we kept their peacefulness for them."

METAMORPHOSIS

(Gene L. Coon)

It was not often that the *Enterprise* needed the services of her shuttlecraft *Galileo,* for usually the Transporter served her purposes better; but this was one of those times. The *Enterprise* had been on other duty when the distress call had come from Epsilon Canaris III, well out of Transporter range, and not even the *Enterprise* could be in two places at once.

Now, however, the *Galileo* was heading back for rendezvous with the mother ship, Kirk at the controls, Spock navigating. The shuttlecraft's passengers were Dr. McCoy and his patient, Assistant Federation Commissioner Nancy Hedford, a very beautiful woman in her early thirties, whose beauty was marred by an almost constant expression of sullenness. The expression did not belie her; she was not a particularly pleasant person to be around.

"We have reached projected point three, Captain," Spock said. "Adjust to new course 201 mark 15."

"Thank you, Mr. Spock . . . Doctor, how is she?"

"No change."

"Small thanks to the Starfleet," Nancy Hedford said.

"Really, Commissioner," McCoy said, "you can't blame the Starfleet—"

"I should have received the proper inoculation ahead of time."

"Sukaro's disease is extremely rare, Commissioner. The chances of anyone contracting it are literally billions to one. How could we predict—"

"I was sent to that planet to prevent a war, Doctor. Thanks to the inefficiency of the medical branch of the Starfleet I have been forced to leave before my job was done. How many millions of innocent people will die because of this so-called rare disease of mine?"

Privately, Kirk was of the opinion that she was over-estimating her own importance; her senior officer could probably handle the situation alone—or maybe even better. But it wouldn't do to say so. "Commissioner, I assure you, once we reach the *Enterprise*, with its medical facilities, we'll have you back on your feet in no time. You'll get back to your job."

"And just how soon will we rendezvous with this ship of yours, Captain?"

"Four hours and twenty-one minutes."

"Captain," Spock said. "The scanners are picking up some kind of small nebulosity ahead. It seems to be—yes, it is on a collision course."

"It can hardly matter," Kirk said, "but we'll swerve for it anyhow."

This, however, proved impossible to do. Every time Kirk changed the *Galileo's* course, the cloud did also. Soon it was within visual distance, a phosphorescent, twisting blob against the immensities of space.

Spock checked the sensors. "It appears to be mostly ionized hydrogen, Captain. But I would say nevertheless that it is not a natural object. It is too dense, changes shape too rapidly, and there is a high degree of electrical activity."

"Whatever it is, we're about to be right in the middle of it."

He had scarcely spoken when the view ahead was completely masked by the glowing, shifting cloud. A moment later, the controls went dead. A quick check showed that communications were out, too.

"Readings, Mr. Spock?"

"Extremely complex patterns of electrical impulses,

and an intense magnetic field—or rather, a number of them. It seems to have locked onto us."

The craft lurched, slightly but definitely. Kirk looked down at his console. "Yes, and it's taking us with it."

"Captain!" the woman's voice called. "What's happening? I demand to know!"

"You already know about as much as we do, Commissioner. Whatever that thing is outside, it's pulling us off our course for the *Enterprise*."

"Now on course 98 mark 12," Spock said. "Heading straight into the Gamma Canaris region."

"Jim!" McCoy said. "We've got to get Miss Hedford to the *Enterprise*—her condition—"

"I'm sorry, Bones. There's nothing we can do."

"I am not at all surprised," Miss Hedford said coldly. "This is exactly the sort of thing I expect from the Starfleet. If I am as sick as this dubious authority claims I am—"

"Believe me, you are," McCoy said. "You may feel fine now, but nevertheless you're very ill."

"Then why are you all just sitting there? I insist—"

"I'm sorry, Commissioner," Kirk said. "We'll do what we can when we can—but right now we're helpless. You might as well sit back and enjoy the ride."

The *Galileo* was put down—there seemed to be no other word for it—on a small planet, of which very few details could be seen through the enveloping nebulosity. But the moment they had grounded, the cloud vanished, leaving them staring out at a broad, deserted sweep of heathlike countryside.

"Bones, Mr. Spock, get some readings on this place." Kirk snapped a switch. "*Enterprise,* this is the *Galileo.* Kirk here. Come in, please. Come in . . . no good, we're not sending. That cloud must still be around someplace. Any data, anybody?"

"The atmosphere is almost identical with that of the Earth," Spock reported, "and so is the gravity. Almost impossible for a planet this small, unless the core is something other than the usual nickel-iron. But suitable for human life."

"Well, I guess we get out and get under," Kirk said.

"Bones, phaser out and maintain full alert. Commissioner, best you stay inside for the time being."

"And just how long a time is that?"

"That's a very good question. I wish I could answer it. Mr. Spock, let's go."

Outside, they went to the rear of the shuttlecraft and unbolted the access panels to the machinery, while McCoy stayed up forward. Checking the works did not take long.

"Very strange," Spock said. "In fact, quite impossible."

"Nothing works."

"Nothing. And for no reason."

"Of course there's a reason. We just haven't found it yet. Let's go over it again."

While they were at it, Nancy Hedford came out and headed for them, looking, as usual, both annoyed and officious. Patience was evidently not her strong point, either. Kirk sighed and straightened.

"Well, Captain?"

"Well, Commissioner?"

"Where is this strange powerful force of yours, which brought us here? Or could it be that you simply made a navigational error?"

"There was no error, Miss Hedford," Kirk said patiently. "For your information, our power units are dead—so I judge that the force you refer to is still in the vicinity."

"I am not interested in alibis, Captain. I insist that you get us off this dismal rock immediately."

"Commissioner, I realize that you're ill, and you're anxious to receive treatment."

"I am anxious, as you put it, to get this medical nonsense out of the way so I can get back to my assignment!"

McCoy, looking rather anxious himself, had joined them. He said, "How do you feel, Commissioner?"

"I wish you would stop asking that stupid question." She strode angrily away.

Kirk managed a rueful grin. "As long as she answers you like that, Bones, I guess she feels all right."

"But she won't for long. The fever's due to hit any time."

As Kirk started to reply, there was a long, hailing call from no very great distance. "Halllooooo!"

They turned, startled. A human figure had emerged from over the horizon, which on this small world was no more than a mile away. It waved its arms, and came toward them at a run.

"Bones, I want a physiological reading on—whoever that is."

The figure disappeared behind a rise, and then appeared at the top of it, looking down on the party. It was a young, sturdy, tall, handsome man in his midthirties, dressed in a one-piece suit of coveralls. His expression was joyful.

"Hello!" he said again, plunging down the rise to them. "Are you real? I mean—I'm not imagining you, am I?"

"We're real enough," Kirk said.

"And you speak English. Earth people?"

Kirk nodded. "From the Federation."

"The Federation? Well, it doesn't matter." He grabbed Kirk's hand enthusiastically. "I'm Cochrane. Been marooned here who knows how long. If you knew how good it was to see you . . . and a woman! A beautiful one at that. Well!"

Kirk made the introductions. Cochrane, still staring at the Commissioner, said, "You're food to a starving man. All of you." He looked over to Spock. "A Vulcan, aren't you. When I was there—hey, there's a nice ship. Simple, clean. Been trying to get her going again? Forget it. It won't work."

He began to circle the shuttlecraft, admiringly. Kirk said in a low voice to McCoy, "Our friend seems to have a grasshopper mind."

"Too many things to take in all at once. Normal reaction. In fact, everything checks out perfectly normal. He's human."

"Mr. Cochrane!" The newcomer rejoined them, still beaming. "We were forced off our course and brought here by some power we couldn't identify—which seems to be here on the surface of the planet at the moment."

"Could be. Strange things happen in space."

"You said we wouldn't be able to get the ship functioning again?" Spock asked.

"Not a chance. Damping field of some sort down here. Power systems don't work. Take my word for it."

"You won't mind if we keep trying?" Spock persisted.

"Go right ahead. You'll have plenty of time."

"How about you, Cochrane?" Kirk said. "What are you doing here?"

"Marooned. I told you. Look, we've got lots of time to learn about each other. I've got a little place not far away. All the comforts of home." He turned to the woman. "I can even offer you a hot bath."

"How acute of you to notice that I needed it," she said icily.

"If you don't mind, Mr. Cochrane," Kirk said, "I'd like a little more than just the statement that you were marooned here. This is a long way off the beaten path."

"That's right. That's why I'm so glad to see you. Look, I'll tell you everything you want to know. But not here." He eyed the shuttlecraft again. "A beauty."

"You've been out of circulation a while. Maybe the principles are new to you. Mr. Spock, would you like to explain our propulsion methods to Mr. Cochrane?"

"Of course, Captain. Mr. Cochrane?"

As the two moved off, McCoy said, "He talks a lot but he doesn't say much."

"I noticed," Kirk said. "And I noticed something else. There's something familiar about him, Bones."

"Familiar? . . . well, now that you mention it, I think so too."

"I can't place him, but . . . how about Miss Hedford?"

"No temperature yet. But we've got to get under way soon. I guarantee you it'll develop."

"You're sure there's no mistake? It is Sakuro's disease?"

"Positive. And something else I'm not mistaken about. Untreated, it's fatal. Always . . . well, what do we do now?"

"I think we'll take Mr. Cochrane up on his offer. At least we can make her comfortable."

Cochrane's house was a simple functional cube, with a door, but no windows. The surrounding area was cultivated.

"You built this, Mr. Cochrane?" Spock said.

"Yes. I had some tools and supplies left over from my crash. It's not Earth, of course, but it's livable. I grow vegetables, as you see. Come on in."

He led the way. The house contained a heating unit which apparently served as a stove, a climate control device, and some reasonably comfortable furniture, all decidedly old. Miss Hedford looked around with distaste.

"What a dreadful, dingy place," she said.

Cochrane only smiled. "But I call it home, Miss Hedford."

"Where did you get the antiques?" Kirk said.

"The antiques? Oh, you mean my gadgets. I imagine things have changed a lot since I wrecked."

"Not that much."

"Must you keep it so terribly hot?" the woman asked.

"The temperature is a constant seventy-two degrees."

"Do you feel hot?" McCoy asked Miss Hedford.

She flopped angrily down in a chair. "I feel infuriated, deeply put upon, absolutely outraged."

"It was quite a hike here," McCoy said. "You're tired. Just take it easy for a while."

"I'll rest later, Doctor. Right now I am planning the report I will make to the Board of Commissioners on the efficiency of the Starfleet. I assure all of you it will be very, very complete."

"Captain! Doctor!" Spock called from the door. "Look at this, please!"

Alarmed at the urgency in his voice, Kirk crossed to the door in one bound. Outside, perhaps half a mile away, was a columnar area of blurry, misty interference, like a tame whirlwind, except that there was no wind. Faint pastel lights and shades appeared and disappeared inside it. With it there was a half sound, half feeling of soft chiming music. For a moment it moved from side to side, gently; then it disappeared.

Kirk turned quickly to Cochrane. "What was that?"

"Sometimes the light plays tricks on you," Cochrane said. "You'd be surprised what I've imagined I've seen around here."

"We imagined nothing, Mr. Cochrane. There was an entity out there, and I suspect it was the same entity that brought us here. Please explain."

"There's nothing to explain."

"Mr. Cochrane, you'll find I have a low tolerance level where the safety of my people are concerned. We find you out here where no human has any business being. We were virtually hijacked in space and brought here—apparently by that thing we just saw out there. I am not just requesting an explanation, Mister. I am demanding it!"

Cochrane shrugged. "All right. Out there—that was the Companion."

"The what?"

"That's what I call it. The fact is, Captain, I did not crash here. I was brought here in my disabled ship. I was almost dead. The Companion saved my life."

"You seem perfectly healthy now," Kirk said. "What was wrong?"

"Old age, Captain. I was eighty-seven years old at the time. I don't know how it did it, but the Companion rejuvenated me. Made me—well—young again, like I am now."

Kirk and Spock exchanged glances. Spock's eyebrows were about to crawl right off the top of his forehead. He said, "I would like to reserve judgment on that part of your story, sir. Would you mind telling us exactly what this Companion of yours is?"

"I told you, I don't know what it is. It exists. It lives. I can communicate with it to a limited extent."

"That's a pretty far-out story," McCoy said.

"You saw the creature. Have you a better story?"

"Mr. Cochrane," Kirk said. "Do you have a first name?"

Cochrane nodded. "Zefram."

McCoy's jaw dropped, but Spock had apparently

81

been expecting the answer. Kirk said, "Cochrane of Alpha Centauri? The discoverer of the space warp?"

"That's right, Captain."

"Zefram Cochrane," McCoy said, "has been dead a hundred and fifty years."

"His body was never found," Spock said.

"You're looking at it, Mr. Spock," Cochrane said.

"You say this Companion of yours found you and rejuvenated you. What were you doing in space at the age of eighty-seven?"

"I was tired, Captain. I was going to die. And I wanted to die in space. That's all."

McCoy turned to Miss Hedford, whose eyes were now closed. He felt her forehead, then took readings. He was obviously concerned by the results.

"These devices," Spock said. "They all date from the time indicated. From your ship, Mr. Cochrane?"

"I cannibalized it. The rest—the food, water, gardens, everything I need—the Companion gives me. Creates it, apparently, out of the native elements."

"If you can communicate with it," Kirk said, "maybe you can find out what *we* are doing here."

"I already know."

"You wouldn't mind telling us?"

"You won't like it."

"We already don't like it."

"You're here to keep me company," Cochrane said. "I was always pretty much of a loner. Spent years in space by myself. At first being alone here didn't bother me. But a hundred and fifty years is a long time, Kirk. Too long. I finally told the Companion I'd die without the company of other humans. I thought it would release me—send me back somehow. Instead, it went out and obviously brought back the first human beings it could find."

"No!" Miss Hedford cried weakly. "No! It's disgusting! We're not animals!"

She began to sob. McCoy, with Kirk's help, lifted her and put her on a cot, where McCoy gave her a shot. Gradually, her sobbing subsided.

"Bad," said McCoy. "Very bad."

"You can't do anything?"

"Keep her quiet. Keep secondary infections from developing. But the attrition rate of her red corpuscles is increasing. I can't stop it."

Kirk turned to Spock. "Mr. Spock, the next time that thing appears, don't fail to get tricorder readings. Find us a weapon to use against that thing."

"Captain, I have already drawn certain tentative conclusions. Considering the anomalously small size of this planet, and the presence of the damping field Mr. Cochrane mentioned, plus the Companion, leads me to believe that it was the moon of some larger body now destroyed, and was colonized by a highly advanced civilization."

"I agree," Cochrane said. "I've found some artifacts which suggest the same thing."

"The point, Spock?"

"One can deduce further that the Companion may be the last survivor of this long-dead culture. You ask me to find a weapon. Do you intend to destroy it?"

"I intend to do whatever is necessary to get us away from here and Commissioner Hedford to a hospital," Kirk said grimly. "If the Companion stands in the way, then we push it out of the way. Clear, Mr. Spock?"

"Quite clear, Captain." Spock picked up his tricorder and left, heading for the shuttlecraft.

"Cochrane, if you left here, what would happen to you?"

"I'd start to age again, normally."

"You want to get away from here?"

"Believe me, Captain, immortality consists largely of boredom. Of course I do . . . what's it like out there? In the galaxy?"

"We're on a thousand planets, and spreading out. We're crossing fantastic distances . . . and finding life everywhere. We estimate there are millions of planets with intelligent life. We haven't begun to map them." Cochrane's eyes were shining. "Interesting?"

"How would you like to go to sleep for a hundred and fifty years and wake up in a new world?"

"Good," Kirk said. "It's all out there, waiting for you. And you'll find your name honored there. But we'll probably need your help to get away."

"You've got it."

"All right. You seem to think this Companion can do almost anything."

"I don't know its limitations."

"Could it cure Commissioner Hedford?"

"I don't know."

"It's worth a try. We're helpless. You say you can communicate with it?"

"To a degree. It's on a non-verbal level, but I usually get my messages across."

"Try it now. See if it can do anything."

Cochrane nodded and stepped outside, followed by Kirk and McCoy. "How do you do it?" Kirk said.

"I just sort of . . . clear my mind. Then it comes. Better stay back."

Cochrane closed his eyes. A long moment passed, and then Kirk heard the melodic humming of the Companion. It appeared near Cochrane, shimmering, resplendent with a dozen beautiful colors, to the sound of faint bells. It moved to Cochrane, enveloped him, gathered around him, hovering. The lights played on Cochrane's face.

"What do you make of that, Bones?" Kirk said softly.

"Almost a symbiosis of some kind. A sort of joining."

"Just what I was thinking. Not exactly like a pet owner speaking to an affectionate animal, would you say?"

"No. More than that."

"I agree. Much more. Possibly . . . love."

Now the Companion was moving away from Cochrane, who was slowly returning to normal. The Companion faded away, and Cochrane shook his head and looked about as if to get his bearings. His eyes settled on Kirk.

"You all right?" Kirk said.

"Oh. Yes. I . . . it always kind of . . . drains me. But I'm all right."

"Well?"

Cochrane shook his head again. "The Companion can't do anything to help Miss Hedford. There seems to be some question of identity involved . . . I didn't understand it. But the answer is no, I'm sure of that."

"Then she'll die."

"Look, I'm sorry. If I could help you, I would. But the Companion won't."

It was several hours before Spock came back from the shuttlecraft. When he returned, he was carrying with him a small but complex black device, obviously in very rough form, as though it had been hastily put together by a gifted child. He took it into the house. "Your weapon, Captain."

"Oho. How does it work?"

"The Companion, as we already know, is mostly plasma—a state of matter characterized by a high degree of ionization. To put the matter simply, it is mostly electricity. I propose to, in effect, short it out. Put this in proximity to the Companion, throw this switch, and we will scramble every electrical impulse the creature can produce. It cannot fail."

Cochrane was staring unhappily at the device. Kirk said, "It troubles you, Cochrane?"

"The Companion saved my life. Took care of me for a hundred and fifty years. We've been . . . very close . . . in a way that's hard to explain. I suppose I even have a sort of affection for it."

"It's also keeping you a prisoner here."

"I don't want it killed."

Spock said, "We may simply render it powerless—"

"But you don't know!" Cochrane said intensely. "You could kill it! I won't stand for that, Kirk."

"We're getting away from here, Cochrane. Make up your mind to that."

"What kind of people are you nowadays?" Cochrane demanded. "Doesn't gratitude mean anything to you?"

"I've got a woman dying in here, Cochrane. I'll do anything I have to to save her life."

Cochrane stared at Kirk, and slowly the fight went out of him. "I suppose, from your point of view, you're right. I only . . ."

"We understand how you feel, Mr. Cochrane," McCoy said. "But it has to be done."

"All right. You want me to call it, I suppose?"

"Please," Kirk said. "Outside."

McCoy remained with his patient. Spock hefted his device, and he and Kirk left the house. Already, Cochrane and the Companion were approaching each other. Soft lights and soft music came from the creature. It almost seemed to be purring.

"Is this close enough?" Kirk whispered.

"I think so," Spock whispered back. "But there is a certain risk. We do not know the extent of the creature's powers."

"Nor it ours. Now, Spock!"

Spock closed the switch. The blurring of the Companion abruptly increased, and a sharp high-pitched humming sound came from it, alarmed, strong. The pastel colors changed to somber blues and greens, and the hint of bells changed to a discordant clanging. Cochrane, only a few feet away from it, grasped his head and staggered, then fell. The evanescent, ever-changing column of plasma swept down upon the house.

Kirk and Spock ducked inside, but there was no safety there. The room was filled with the whirling and clanging. With it, Kirk felt a terrible sense of pressure, all over his body. The breath was crushed out of him. He struck out, but there was nothing to strike at. Beside him, he was aware that Spock had dropped the device and was also gasping futilely for air.

"Stop it! Stop it!" McCoy's voice shouted, as if from a great distance. "It's killing them!"

Cochrane came in, and, immediately divining what was happening, went into the position of communion. The Companion's colors returned to the pastel, and the creature faded away. Kirk and Spock both fell to their knees, gulping in great gasps of air. McCoy knelt beside them; Cochrane went out again.

"Are you all right?" McCoy said. "Can you breathe?"

Kirk nodded. "All . . . right, Bones." He got shakily to his feet, followed by Spock, who also seemed to be regaining his strength rapidly. "Cochrane's got it off us. I don't know whether he did us a favor or not."

"What kind of talk is that?" McCoy said sharply.

"How do you fight a thing like that? I've got a ship

86

somewhere out there ... the responsibility for four lives here ... and one of them dying."

"That's not your fault."

"I'm in command, Bones. That makes it my fault. Now I've had it. I can't destroy it. I can't force it to let us go."

After a moment McCoy said, "You're a soldier so often that maybe you forget you were also trained to be a diplomat. Why not try using a carrot instead of a stick?"

"But what could I offer ... Hmmm. Maybe we can. Spock!"

"Yes, Captain."

"The universal translator on the shuttlecraft. We can try that. Talk to the thing."

"The translator is for use with more congruent life-forms."

"Adjust it. Change it. The trouble with immortality is that it's boring. Adjusting the translator would give you something to do."

"It's possible. If I could widen its pattern of reception—"

"Right down your alley, Mr. Spock. Get it here and get to work."

The translator was small but intricate. Cochrane eyed it interestedly, while McCoy tended his patient. "How does that gadget work?" he said.

"There are certain universal ideas and concepts, common to all intelligent life," Kirk explained. "This device instantaneously compares the frequency of brain-wave patterns, selects those it recognizes, and provides the necessary grammar and vocabulary."

"You mean the box speaks?"

"With the voice, or its approximation, of whatever creature is on the sending end. It's not perfect, of course, but it usually works well enough. Are you ready, Mr. Spock?"

"Quite ready, Captain."

"Mr. Cochrane, call the Companion, please."

Cochrane left the house, Kirk and Spock once more following, with the translator. And again the sound of the Companion preceded its appearance; then it was there, misty, enigmatic. Spock touched the translator and nodded to Kirk.

"Companion . . . we wish to talk to you."

There was a change in the sound. The Companion drew away from Cochrane. Then a voice came from the translator. It was soft, gentle—and unmistakably feminine.

"How can we communicate? My thoughts . . . you are hearing them. This is interesting."

"Feminine, Spock," Kirk said. "No doubt about it."

"Odd. The matter of gender could change the entire situation."

"Dr. McCoy and I are way ahead of you, Mr. Spock."

"Then it is not a zoo-keeper."

"No, Mr. Spock. A lover . . . Companion! It is wrong to hold us here against our will."

"The man needs the company of his own kind, or he will cease to exist," the gentle voice said. "He felt it to me."

"One of us is about to cease to exist. She must be taken to a place where we can care for her."

"The man needs others of his species. That is why you are here. The man must continue."

"Captain, there is a peculiar, dispassionate logic here," Spock said. "Pragmatism unalloyed. From its words, I would say it will never understand our point of view."

"Maybe. Companion, try to understand. It is the nature of our species to be free, just as it is your nature to stay here. We will cease to exist in captivity."

"Your bodies have stopped their peculiar degeneration. You will continue without end. There will be sustenance. There will be nothing to harm you. You will continue and the man will continue. This is necessary."

"Captain!" Spock said. "This is a marvelous opportunity for us to add to our knowledge. Ask it about its nature, its history—"

"Mr. Spock, this is no classroom. I'm trying to get us away from here."

"A chance like this may never come again. It could tell us so much—"

"Mr. Spock, get lost. Companion, it is plain you do not understand us. This is because you are not of our species. Believe me, we do not lie. What you offer us is not continuation. It is non-existence. We will cease to exist. Even the man will cease to exist."

"Your impulses are illogical. This communication is useless. The Man must continue. Therefore, you will continue. It is necessary."

The voice fell silent. The Companion moved away. Slowly it started to grow fainter, and finally was not there at all.

Kirk's shoulders sagged, and he went back into the house, followed by Spock. Cochrane came in after them.

"Captain," he said, "why did you build that translator of yours with a feminine voice box?"

"We didn't," Kirk said.

"But I heard—"

"The ideas of male and female are universal constants, Cochrane. The Companion is definitely female."

"I don't understand."

"You don't?" said McCoy. "A blind man could see it with his cane. You're not a pet, Cochrane. Nor a specimen kept in a cage. You're a lover."

"I'm—what?"

"Isn't it evident?" Kirk said. "Everything she does is for you. Provides for you. Feeds you. Shelters you. Clothes you. Brings you companions when you're lonely."

"Her attitude, when she approaches you, is profoundly different from when she contacts us," Spock added. "In appearance, in sound, in method. Though I do not completely understand the emotion, it obviously exists. The Companion loves you."

Cochrane stared at them. "That's—that's ridiculous!"

"Not at all," Kirk said. "We've seen similar situations."

"But after a hundred and fifty years—"

"What happens when you communicate with it?" Spock said.

"Why, we sort of . . . it—it merges with my mind."

"Of course. It is nothing to be shocked by. A simple symbolic union of two minds."

"That's outrageous! Do you know what you're saying? No, you couldn't! But . . . all the years . . . letting something . . . as alien as that . . . into my mind, my feelings—" Suddenly Cochrane was furious as well as astonished. "It tricked me! It's some kind of an . . . emotional vampire! Crawling around inside me!"

"It didn't hurt you, did it?" Kirk said.

"Hurt me? What has that to do with it? You can be married to a woman you love for fifty years and still keep your private places in your mind. But this—this thing—fed on me!"

"An interesting attitude," Spock said. "Typical of your time, I should say, when humanity had much less contact with alien life-forms than at present."

"Don't sit there and calmly analyze a disgusting thing like this!" Cochrane exploded. "What kind of men are you, anyway?"

"There's nothing disgusting about it, Cochrane," McCoy said. "It's just one more life-form. You get used to these things."

"You turn my stomach! You're as bad as it is!"

"I fail to understand your highly emotional reaction," Spock said. "Your relationship with the Companion was, for a hundred and fifty years, emotionally satisfying, eminently practical, and totally harmless. It may, indeed, have been quite beneficial."

Cochrane glared at them. "So this is what the future looks like—men who don't have the slightest notion of decency or morality. Well, maybe I'm a hundred and fifty years out of style, but I'm not going to be fodder for some inhuman—monstrous—" Choking up, he swung on his heel and walked out.

"A most parochial attitude," Spock said.

"Doctor," Nancy Hedford's voice called weakly. "Doctor."

McCoy hurried to her, Kirk following. "Right here, Miss Hedford."

She managed a very faint, almost bitter laugh. "I . . . heard him. He was loved . . . and he resents it."

"You rest," McCoy said.

"No. I don't want . . . want to die . . . I've been . . . good at my job, Doctor. But I've . . . never been loved. What kind . . . of a life is that? Not to be loved . . . never . . . and now I'm dying. And he . . . runs away from love . . ."

She fell silent, gasping for breath. McCoy's eyes were grim.

"Captain," Spock called from the door. "Look out here."

Outside, the Companion was back, looking much the same as usual, but Cochrane was standing away from it, barely controlling himself, icily furious.

"Do you understand?" he was saying. "I don't want anything to do with you."

The Companion moved a little closer, chiming questioningly, insistently. Cochrane backed away.

"I said keep away! You'll never get close enough to trick me again! Stay away from me! I know you understand me! Stay away! Leave me alone, from now on!"

Shaken, white-faced and sweating, Cochrane came back to his house. Kirk turned back to McCoy. Nancy was lying quite still.

"Bones? Is it over?"

"No. But she's moribund. Respiration highly erratic. Blood pressure dropping. She'll be dead in ten minutes. And I—"

"You did everything you could, Bones."

"Are you sorry for her, Kirk?" Cochrane said, still in an icy rage. "Are you really feeling something? Don't bother. Because that's the only way any of us are going to get away from here. By dying!"

An idea, a forlorn hope, came to Kirk. He picked up the translator and went outside. The Companion was still there.

"Companion. Do you love the man?"

"I do not understand," said the feminine voice from the translator.

"Is he important to you—more important than anything? Is it as though he were part of you?"

"He is part of me. He must continue."

"But he will not continue. He will cease to exist. By

your feeling for him you are condemning him to an existence he will find unbearable."

"He does not age. He remains forever."

"You refer to his body," said Kirk. "I speak of his spirit. Companion, inside the shelter a female of our species lies dying. She will not continue. That is what will happen to the man unless you release all of us."

"I do not understand."

"Our species can only survive when there are obstacles to overcome. You take away all obstacles. Without them to strengthen us, we weaken and die. You regard the man only as a toy. You only amuse yourself with him."

"You are wrong," said the translator. Was there urgency as well as protest in that voice? "The man is the center of all things. I care for him."

"But you can't really love him. You don't have the slightest knowledge of love—of the total union of two people. You are the Companion; he is the man; you are two different things, and can never join. You can never know love. You may keep him here forever, but you will always be separate, apart from him."

There was a long pause. Then the Companion said, "If I were human . . . there can be love . . ."

Then the creature faded from sight. Kirk went back into the shelter, almost bumping into McCoy, who had been standing behind him. "What did you hope to gain by that?" the surgeon said.

"Convince her of the hopelessness of it. The emotion of love frequently expresses itself in sacrifice. If love is what she feels, she might let him go."

"But she—or it—is inhuman, Captain," Spock said. "You cannot expect her to react like a human."

"I can try."

"It won't do any good," Cochrane said. "I know."

From the direction of the cot, a voice said, "Zefram Cochrane." It was Nancy's voice, clear and strong, but somehow as if the use of human lips, tongue and vocal cords had become unfamiliar. They all spun around.

There stood Nancy Hedford—but transformed, radiant, soft, gentle, staring at Cochrane. The rosy glow of health was evident in her cheek. McCoy raised his medical tricorder and stared at it, thunderstruck, but Kirk had no need to ask what he saw. The Nancy Hedford who had been about to die was not sick at all now.

"Zefram Cochrane," she said. "We are understanding."

"It's—it's her!" Cochrane said. "Don't you understand? It's the Companion!"

"Yes," said Nancy. "We are here—those you knew as the Commissioner and the Companion. We are both here."

Spock said, "Companion, you do not have the power to create life."

"No. That is for the maker of all things."

"But Commissioner Hedford was dying."

"That part of us was too weak to hold on. In a moment there would have been no continuing. Now we are together. Now we understand that which you called love—both of us. It fills a great need. That we did not have, we now have."

"You mean—you're both there in one body?" Kirk said.

"We are one. There is so much hunger, so much wanting." She moved toward Cochrane, who retreated a step. "Poor Zefram Cochrane. We frighten you. We never frightened you before." Tears formed in her eyes. "Loneliness. This is loneliness. We know loneliness. What a bitter thing. Zefram Cochrane, how do you bear it?"

"How do you know what loneliness is?" Cochrane said.

"To wear this form is to discover pain." She extended a hand. "Let us touch you, Zefram Cochrane."

His hand slowly went out, and they touched.

Kirk turned his head and said in a low voice: "Spock. Check out the shuttlecraft. The engines, communication, everything."

"We hear you, Captain," Nancy said. "It is not necessary. Your vehicle will operate as before. So will your communications device."

"You're letting us go?" Cochrane said.

"We would do nothing to stop you. Captain, you

said that we would not know love because we were not human. Now we are human, all human, and nothing more. We will know the change of the days. We will know death. But to touch the hand of the man—nothing is as important. Is this happiness, Zefram Cochrane? When the sun is warmer? The air sweeter? The sounds of this place like gentle currents in the air?"

"You are very beautiful," Cochrane said in a low voice.

"Part of me understands. Part does not. But it pleases me."

"I could explain. Many things. It'll be an eye-opener to you." He was alive with excitement. "A thousand worlds, a thousand races. I'll show you everything— just as soon as I learn my way around again. Maybe I can make up for everything you did for me."

Sadness appeared in Nancy's eyes. "I cannot go with you, Zefram Cochrane."

Cochrane was stunned. "Of course you can. You have to."

"My life emanates from this place. If I leave it, for more than a tiny march of days, I will cease to exist. I must return, even as you must consume matter to maintain your life."

"But—you have powers—you can—"

"I have become almost as you. The march of days will affect me. But to leave here would mean a cessation of my existence."

"You mean you gave up everything to become human?"

"It is nothing . . . compared to the touch of you."

"But you'll age, like any other human. Eventually you'll die."

"The joy of this hour is enough. I am pleased."

"I can't fly off and leave you here," Cochrane said. "You saved my life. You took care of me and you loved me. I never understood, but I do now."

"You must be free, Zefram Cochrane."

Kirk said gently: "The *Galileo* is waiting, Mr. Cochrane."

"But . . . If I take her away from here, she'll die. If I

94

leave her . . . she's human. She'll die of loneliness. And that's not all. I love her. Is that surprising?"

"Not coming from a human being," Spock said. "You are, after all, essentially irrational."

Cochrane put his arms around her. "I can't leave her. And this isn't such a bad place. I'm used to it."

"Think it over, Mr. Cochrane," Kirk said. "There's a galaxy out there, waiting to honor you."

"I have honors enough. She loves me."

"But you will age, both of you," Spock said. "There will be no more immortality. You will grow old here, and finally die."

"That's been happening to men and women for a long time . . . and I've got the feeling that it's one of the pleasanter things about being human—as long as you do it together."

"You're sure?" Kirk said.

"There's plenty of water. The climate is good for growing things. I might even try to plant a fig tree. Every man's entitled to that, isn't he?" He paused, then added soberly, "It isn't gratitude, Captain. Now that I see her, touch her, I know. I love her. We'll have a lot of years, and they'll be happy ones."

"Mr. Cochrane, you may or may not be doing the right thing. But I wish you the best. Mr. Spock, Bones, let's go."

As they turned, Cochrane said, "Captain."

"Yes?"

"Don't tell them about Cochrane. Let it go."

Kirk smiled. "Not a word, Mr. Cochrane."

As they settled into the *Galileo*, Spock said, "I pose you an interesting question, Captain. Have we not aided in the commission of bigamy? After all, the Companion and Commissioner Hedford are now sharing the same body."

"Now you're being parochial, Mr. Spock," McCoy said. "Bigamy is not everywhere illegal. Besides, Nancy Hedford was all but dead. Only the Companion is keeping her alive. If it withdrew, Nancy wouldn't last ten minutes. In fact, I'm going to report her dead as soon as we hit the *Enterprise*."

"Besides, what difference does it make?" Kirk said. "Love was the one thing Nancy and the Companion wanted most. Now they have it."

"But not for eternity," McCoy said. "Only a lifetime."

"Yes. But that's enough, Bones. For humans."

"That's a very illogical remark, Jim." As Spock's eyebrows climbed, McCoy added, "However, it happens to be true."

Kirk grinned and raised his communicator. "Kirk to *Enterprise*."

The communicator fairly shouted back. "Captain! This is Scotty. Are you all right?"

"We're perfectly all right. Can you get a fix on us?"

"Computing now . . . yes, locked on."

"Very good. I'll continue transmission. Assume standard orbit on arrival. We'll transfer up on the shuttle-craft."

"But what happened, Captain?"

"Not very much, in the end," Kirk said. "Only the oldest story in the world."

THE DEADLY YEARS

(David P. Harmon)

There was no sign of Robert Johnson when the party from the *Enterprise* materialized on Gamma Hydra IV. In fact, there was no sign of anybody, and their arrival site, which otherwise resembled a Kansas field in mid-August, was eerily silent.

There were the overbright sun, the varied greens of leaves and grasses, even the shimmer of heat waves over the adjacent meadow. But all sounds of life were missing —insect, animal, human. All that suggested that it was the specified headquarters of the Johnson expedition was a scattering of pre-fab buildings.

Spock, Kirk noted, was looking troubled too. McCoy said, "Perhaps they weren't expecting us."

Spock shook his head. "Our arrival was scheduled well in advance, Doctor. An annual check of every scientific expedition is routine."

"Besides, I had sub-space contact with the leader of this expedition, a Robert Johnson, not an hour ago," Kirk said.

"Did he report anything wrong, Jim?"

"No . . . and yet there was *something* wrong. I can't quite nail it down, but his conversation was disjointed, somehow, as though he were having trouble sticking to the subject, or was worried about something." Kirk pointed at the nearest building. "Mr. Chekov, check that place. Mr. Spock and I will check that one. McCoy, Scotty, Lieutenant Galway, look around, see if you can find anyone."

The group broke up. Arlene Galway was looking a little scared, Kirk thought. Well, this was only her first extra-solar planet; she'd toughen in due course. And the circumstances were a little odd.

Kirk and Spock were about to enter "their" building when a scream rent the air. Whirling, Kirk saw Chekov bursting out into the open, looking about wildly.

"Captain! Captain!" Chekov's voice had gone up a full octave. Kirk loped forward and grabbed him.

"What's wrong?"

"Captain! In there!"

"Control yourself, Ensign! What is it?"

"A man, sir! In there!" Cheokov seemed a little calmer. "A dead man."

"All right, we'll check it. But why the panic? You've seen dead men before."

"I know," Chekov said, a little ashamedly. "But this one's, uh, peculiar, and frankly, sir, it startled me."

" 'Scared' might be the better word. All right, Bones, Spock, let's take a look." Kirk drew his phaser.

The interior of the building was quite dark—not black, but Kirk, coming in from the bright sunlight, had trouble getting used to it. At first, the building seemed quite empty; then he saw some sort of low structure near its end. He approached cautiously.

Then he abruptly understood what had panicked the unprepared Chekov. The object was a crudely constructed wooden coffin, for which two sawhorses served as a catafalque.

The body it held might have been Methuselah's. Deep wrinkles made its facial features also indecipherable. The open mouth was toothless, its near-white gums shriveled, its eyes sunk in caverns, flattened under their lids of flabby skin. The body seemed to be mere bones, barely held together by a brown-spotted integument of tissue-paper thinness. Clawed hands were crossed on its collapsed chest.

Chekov's voice said through the dimness, "I bumped into it walking backward, sir, and I—"

"I quite understand, Ensign. Rest easy. Bones, what's this?"

"Exactly what it looks like, Jim. Death by natural causes—in other words, old age."

"Doctor," Spock said, "I ran a personnel check on the members of this expedition before we beamed-down, and I can assure you that not one of them was . . ."

Midway through this sentence Kirk became aware of the shuffling of feet outside the open door. They all turned as Spock's voice trailed off.

A man and woman tottered toward them, supporting themselves with sticks. They were stooped and shrunken, the skin of their skulls showing through their thin white hair.

The man said, in a quavering voice, "They've come to pay their respects to Professor Alvin."

"I am Captain Kirk of the—"

"You'll have to speak louder," the man said, cupping his ear with his free hand.

"I said I am Captain Kirk of the *Enterprise*. Who are you?"

"Robert Johnson," said the old man, nodding. "And this is my wife Elaine."

"That's impossible," Kirk said. "The Johnsons are— how old are you?"

"Me? I'm . . . let me see . . . oh yes, I'm twenty-nine. Elaine is twenty-seven."

The shocked silence was at last broken by McCoy. "I am a physician. You both need rest and medical care."

There were only three decrepit survivors of the expedition to be beamed-up to Sickbay and Nurse Chapel's gentle but efficient care. Standing beside McCoy, Kirk leaned over Robert Johnson's bed.

"Can you hear me, Dr. Johnson?"

The filmed eyes found his face. "Not deaf yet, you know. Not yet."

"Have you any idea what happened?"

"What happened?" Johnson echoed vaguely.

"Did your instruments show anything?"

The old mind was wandering. As though appealing to some benevolent but absent god, Johnson said, "Elaine was so beautiful . . . so beautiful."

"He can hear you, Jim, but he can't understand. Let him rest."

Kirk nodded. "Nurse Chapel, if any of them seem lucid, we'll be in the briefing room." He went to the intercom. "Kirk to bridge. Mr. Spock, Commodore Stocker, Dr. Wallace, to the briefing room, please. Bones, I'll ask you to come along."

Janet Wallace and George Stocker were distinguished guests; he an able administrator in his mid-forties, she an endocrinologist, in her late twenties and extremely attractive. They were waiting with Spock at the big table when he and McCoy arrived. He nodded to them all and sat down himself. "Commodore Stocker, I've asked you to this briefing because Gamma Hydra Four falls within the area of your administration."

Trim, competent-looking, the tall man said, "I appreciate that, Captain."

The merest hint of constraint came into Kirk's voice as he spoke to the dark-eyed girl who sat next to the Commodore. "Dr. Wallace, though you are a new member of our crew, your credentials as an endocrinologist are impressive. In this situation we face, I'd appreciate your working closely with Dr. McCoy."

She smiled at him. "Yes, Captain."

He turned hastily to McCoy. "Fill them in, Bones."

McCoy said, "The survivors of the expedition to Gamma Hydra Four are not merely suffering from extreme old age. They are getting older, much older by the minute. My examinations have shown up nothing. I haven't a clue to the cause of this rapidly aging process."

"Mr. Spock, what about environment and atmosphere?"

"Sensors show nothing inimical to human life, sir. The atmosphere screens out the usual amount of harmful cosmic rays."

"We are close, though," Kirk said, "to the neutral zone between our Federation and the Romulan Confederation. The Romulans may have a new weapon.

Perhaps they have been using members of the expedition as guinea pigs."

"I have begun to investigate that possibility, Captain," Spock said.

Kirk rose. "I want you all to check out everything in your particular specialties. No matter how remote, how far-fetched seems the notion, I want it run down." He paused for emphasis. "We will remain in orbit until we have the answer."

Stocker spoke. "I am anxious to get to Star Base Ten in order to assume my new post. I am sure you understand that, Captain."

"I will do what I can to see that you make your due date, Commodore."

"Thank you, Captain."

The men, pushing back their chairs, left the briefing room. But the dark-eyed Dr. Wallace didn't move. Kirk turned at the door. "Anything I can do for you, Doctor?"

"Yes," she said. "You might, for instance, say 'Hello, Janet'. You might be a little less the cold, efficient starship captain and a little more the old . . . friend."

"Janet, as captain, I have certain—my duties are heavy." Then he gave her a wry little smile. "Or maybe I just don't want to get burned again."

"I'm carrying a little scar tissue of my own," she said.

There was a small silence. Then he said, "How long has it been?"

"More than six years, Jim."

"A long time. But there wouldn't be any change if we started it up all over again, would there? I've got my ship; and you've got your work. Neither of us will change."

"You never asked why I married after we called it off."

"I supposed you'd found another man you loved."

"I found a man I admired."

"And in the same field as you. You didn't have to give up anything."

"No, I didn't. But he's dead now, Jim."

She went to him, her hands extended. Kirk hesitated.

101

Then he took one of the hands, his eyes searching the warm brown ones—and Uhura's voice spoke on the intercom.

"Captain Kirk, Mr. Spock would like to see you on the bridge."

"Tell Mr. Spock I'm on my way." He was finding deeper depths in the brown eyes. "Janet, we're under pressure right now. Maybe, when it eases off, things will be—"

Uhura's voice interrupted again. "Captain Kirk, Mr. Scott would like to see you in Engineering."

"Tell him I'll be down after I check with Mr. Spock." He drew Janet closer to him. Lifting her chin, he said, "But this time there must be truth between us. You and I, with our eyes open, knowing what each of us are."

"It's been a long six years," she said; and placed her arms around his neck. He had bent his head to her mouth when the intercom spoke for the third time. "Captain Kirk!"

"On my way, Lieutenant Uhura." A sudden wave of weariness swept over him. He touched the girl's mouth with his forefinger. "Six long years—and that intercom is trying to make it six more. Dr. Wallace, your lips are as tempting as ever—but as I remarked, my duties are heavy."

The weariness stayed with him on his way to the bridge. Sulu greeted him with a "Standard orbit, Captain." He said, "Maintain" and crossed to Spock at the computer station.

"I have rechecked the sensors, sir. Gamma Hydra Four checks out as a Class M planet, nitrogen-oxygen atmosphere, normal mass with conventional atmospheric conditions. I can find nothing at all out of the ordinary."

"How about that comet that recently passed through here?"

"I am running checks on it, sir. As yet I have no conclusions. The comet is a rogue and has never been investigated."

"Captain Kirk!"

It was Stocker. He looked like a man with a determined idea. "Facilities at Star Base Ten," he said, "are much more complete than those on board ship. It seems to me your investigations would be facilitated by proceeding there at once. I assure you of every cooperation."

"Thank you, Commodore; but we have a few facilities of our own. I am going to Engineering, Mr. Spock." He left the computer station to say to Sulu, "Maintain standard orbit, Mr. Sulu."

Surprised, Sulu exclaimed, "But you already gave that order, sir!"

Kirk looked surprised himself. "Did I? Oh, well. Follow it."

As he left the bridge, Spock stared after him, a look of concern in his eyes.

Lieutenant Galway appeared uneasy, too, as she opened the door of Sickbay. "Dr. McCoy, can I speak with you a moment?"

"Of course." He motioned her to a chair but she didn't take it. "I know," she said, "that this is going to sound foolish. But—I seem to be having a little trouble hearing."

"Probably nothing important," McCoy said.

"I never had any trouble before."

"I'll have a look at you. Maybe a simple hypersonic treatment will clear it up." She said, "Thank you, Doctor" and followed him into the examination room.

Kirk was discovering some trouble of his own. Alone in his quarters, stripped to the waist, he dried the face he'd just shaved, and reached for the clean shirt he'd laid out on the bed. As he raised his right arm to insert it into a sleeve, a sharp stab of pain struck his right shoulder. He winced, lowered the arm, flexed it, massaging the shoulder muscle. The pain persisted. Slowly, carefully, he put on the shirt. Then he moved to the intercom and flicked a button. "Progress report, Mr. Spock?"

"All research lines negative, Captain."

Kirk said, "Astronomical section reports that a comet recently passed by. Check into that."

Spock waited a moment before he replied, "I'm doing that, sir, according to your order. We discussed it earlier."

"Oh. Well, let me know what you come up with. I'll be in Sickbay."

"Yes, Captain."

The walk to Sickbay seemed longer than usual. The pain in the right shoulder had extended to the right knee. There was a slight trace of a limp in Kirk's movement as he entered Sickbay. In its bed section, all but one of the three beds was vacant. He thought, "So two of the rescued Johnson party are gone." It was a depressing reflection. Then he saw Nurse Chapel draw a blanket up and over the face of the patient who occupied the third bed.

McCoy looked up. "Robert Johnson, deceased. The last one, Jim. Cause of death—old age."

"You did what you could," Kirk said.

The intercom spoke. "Dr. McCoy? This is Scott. Can I come up and see you?"

McCoy answered shortly. "You just need vitamins. But yes, come up anyway, Scotty."

He punched off and Kirk said, "Bones, I believe you're getting gray!"

"You take over my job and see what it does to you!" Low-voiced, McCoy gave an order to Nurse Chapel. Then he turned back to Kirk. "Well, what's *your* problem?"

"My shoulder," Kirk said. "Got a little twinge in it. Probably just a muscle strain."

"Probably, Dr. Kirk," McCoy snapped.

Kirk grinned. "Reprimand noted, sir. Okay, no more diagnoses by me."

McCoy ran his Feinberger over Kirk's shoulder. He frowned. "Hmmm. Maybe we'd better run a complete check on you."

"Well? Muscle strain?"

McCoy shook his head. "No, Jim. It's an advanced case of arthritis. And spreading."

"But that's not possible!"

"I'll run the check again, but I'll get the same answer."

He didn't run it again. For Kirk, his dismay still on his face was staring past him at the Sickbay door. Mc-

Coy turned. Scott stood there—a Scott with snow-white hair who appeared to be sixty years of age.

Sickbay on the *Enterprise* had become a section that seemed to have been appropriated by a Golden Age club. Assembled there on Kirk's order were every member of the crew who had contacted Gamma Hydra Four. With the single exception of Chekov, each one had been affected by the rapidly aging process. Kirk looked fifty-five: McCoy ten years older. Nor had Spock's Vulcan heritage been entirely able to immunize him against its effects. Wrinkles cracked his face; the skin under his eyes had gone baggy. Lieutenant Galway might have been a woman in her mid-sixties. Scott looked oldest of them all.

"All right, Bones," Kirk said. "Let's have it."

McCoy said, "All of us who went down to the planet, except Ensign Chekov, are aging rapidly. The rates vary from person to person, but it averages thirty years each day. I don't know what's causing it—virus, bacteria or evil spirits. I'm trying to find out."

"Spock? I asked you for some calculations."

"Based on what Dr. McCoy gave me, I'd say that we each have a week to live. It would also seem that since our mental faculties are aging faster than our bodies, we will become little better than mental vegetables in less time than a week."

"You mean total senility?"

"Yes, Captain. In a very short time!"

Kirk took a step away from the group. "What a . . . a filthy way to die!" He turned slowly, accommodating his aching knee. "I want every research facility on this ship, every science technician, to immediately start round-the-clock research. I want the answer! And a remedy! And you might start in by telling me why Chekov wasn't affected!"

"I'm doing what I can," McCoy said. He removed his Feinberger diagnostic instrument from Spock. "You are disgustingly healthy, Spock."

"I must differ with you, Doctor. I am finding it difficult to concentrate. My eyesight appears to be failing.

And the normal temperature of the ship strikes me as increasingly cold."

"I didn't say you were not affected."

Scott said dully, "Can I go back to my station?"

"Feel up it it, Scotty?" Kirk asked.

"Of course I do. Just need a little rest, that's all."

McCoy said, "You can leave too if you wish, Lieutenant Galway."

She didn't move. McCoy spoke louder. "Lieutenant Galway?"

"What? You spoke to me, Doctor?"

"Yes. I said you could go. Why not go to your quarters and get some sleep?"

"No! I don't want to sleep! Can't you understand? If I sleep . . . what will I find when I wake up?"

Kirk said, "Lieutenant Galway, report to your station and continue with your duties."

Her "Yes, sir" was grateful. She rose painfully from her chair, moved toward the door, and came face to face with herself in a mirror. She turned from it in anger.

"What a stupid place to hang a mirror!"

She half-stumbled out. Kirk looked after her. "She's seven or eight years younger than I am. She looks ten years older."

"People normally age at different speeds, Jim."

Kirk pointed to Chekov. "But why hasn't he aged?"

"I don't know."

"Well, I want to know! Is it his youth? His blood type? His glands? His medical history? His genes?"

"Nurse Chapel, prepare Mr. Chekov for a complete physical."

She rose. "Come along, Ensign. This won't hurt. Much."

As the door closed behind the nurse and the reluctant Chekov, Janet Wallace turned to McCoy. "A few years ago on Aldebaran Three, my husband and I used a variation of cholesterol block to slow arteriosclerosis in animals."

"Did it work?"

"Sometimes. But the side effects were fierce. We gave it up."

"Try it anyhow, Dr. Wallace. Try anything, but do it quickly!"

"Yes, sir." She went out in turn.

"Mr. Spock, return to the bridge," Kirk said. "I'll join you shortly. Keep me posted on Chekov, Bones."

He found Janet Wallace waiting for him in the corridor. "I thought you were on your way to the biochemistry lab, Doctor."

"We both go in the same direction, Jim."

After a moment, he nodded. "So we do."

She adjusted her pace to his slower walk. "We know the problem," she said. "We know the effects it is having. And we know the progress of the affliction. Therefore, once we find the proper line of research, it's only logical that we find the solution."

Kirk smiled. "You sound like my First Officer."

"No problem, Jim—not even ours—is insoluble."

"I could name you five insoluble problems right off the top of my head. For example, why was the universe created? How can we trust what we think we know? Is there such a thing as an invariably right or wrong action? What is the nature of beauty? What is the proof of Fermat's last theorem? None of those are soluble by logic."

"No. The heart is not a logical organ. Our . . . situation . . . doesn't have its roots in logic." She put her arm through his. "When I married Theodore Wallace, I thought I was over you. I was wrong."

Kirk gave her a sharp look. "When did you realize this? Today?"

"What?"

"How much older was your husband than you?"

"What difference does it make?" she asked.

"Answer me!"

"Twenty-six years," she told him reluctantly. Then, as though he'd demanded an explanation, she added, "He was a brilliant man . . . we were stationed on a lonely outpost . . . working together—" She broke off to cry, "Jim, I don't want to talk about him! I want to talk about us!"

"Look at me!" Kirk demanded. He seized her shoulders. "I said look at me! What do you see?"

107

"I—I see Captain James Kirk," she said unsteadily. "A man of morality, decency—strong, handsome—"

"And *old!*" he cried. "Old—and getting older every minute!"

"Jim, please . . ."

"What are you offering me, Jan? Love—or a goodbye present?"

"That's very cruel," she said.

"It's honest!" His voice was harsh with bitterness. "Just stay around for two more days, Janet! By that time I'll really be old enough for your love!"

Young Chekov was feeling the strain of multiple medical examinations. "Give us some more blood, Chekov!" he muttered to Sulu. "The needle won't hurt, Chekov! Take off your shirt, Chekov! Roll over, Chekov! Breathe deeply, Chekov! Blood sample! Marrow sample! Skin sample! They take so many samples of me I'm not even sure I'm here!"

"You'll live," Sulu said.

"Oh yes, I'll live . . . but I won't enjoy—"

Kirk entered the bridge and he fell silent. Sulu said, "Maintaining standard orbit, Captain."

"Increase orbit to twenty thousand perigee."

As Kirk moved to his command chair, Yeoman Doris Atkins handed him a clipboard. "Will you sign this, sir?" He glanced at the board, scribbled his name on it and was handing it back to her when Commodore Stocker approached him.

"I hope to have a few words with you, Captain."

"I have very little time, Commodore."

"Very well, sir. I just want to remind you we have a due date at Star Base Ten."

"I'm afraid we'll be late for it, Commodore Stocker. I do not intend to leave this area until we have found a solution to our problem."

"Captain, I am watching four very valuable, and one almost irreplaceable, members of the Starfleet failing before my eyes. I want to do something to help."

"If you are so concerned," Kirk said, "I'll send a sub-space message to Star Base Ten and explain the situation."

At his computer station, Spock shook his head. Kirk noticed the gesture. "Yes, Mr. Spock?"

"Captain . . . you sent such a message this morning."

"Oh. Yes, of course." He changed the subject. "Yeoman Atkins."

"Sir?"

"Where's the report on fuel consumption?"

"You just signed it, sir."

"If I'd signed it, I wouldn't have asked for it! Give it to me!"

The girl timidly handed him the board. There was his signature. Angrily, he handed the board back to her and sank down in his command chair. He saw Chekov and Sulu exchange looks. Uhura's back was resolutely turned.

Kirk closed his eyes. *I need rest. You can take just so much. Then you've had it.* He was helpless; that was the fact. And he had never been so tired before in all his life . . . worry, despair . . . they weren't going to change a thing . . . tired . . . tired . . .

As from a great distance, he heard Spock's voice. "Captain! I believe I know the cause! I decided to—" The voice stopped, and Kirk let his mind drift again; but then he was being shaken. "Captain!" He roused himself with immense effort.

"Hmm? Spock? Sorry . . . I was thinking."

"Understandable, sir."

"Um. Do you have something to report, Mr. Spock?"

"Yes, sir. I think I know the cause of the affliction. I cannot be sure, but the lead I have seems very promising."

Alert now, Kirk said, "What is it?"

"The comet," Spock said. "The orbit of Gamma Hydra Four carried it directly through the comet's tail. I examined the residue on conventional radiation setting and discovered nothing. But when I reset our sensors at the extreme lower range of the scale, undetected radiation appeared. Below normal radiation readings . . . but definitely present. And undoubtedly residue from the comet's tail."

"Good, Mr. Spock. Let's get that to Dr. McCoy immediately."

Pain stabbed in his right knee as he rose. He massaged it and limped over to Uhura. "Lieutenant, take a message to Starfleet Command."

"Yes, sir."

"Because of the proximity of the Romulans, use Code Two."

"But, sir, the Romulans have broken Code Two. If you will remember the last bulletin——"

"Then use Code Three!"

"Yes, sir. Code Three."

"Message. Key to affliction may be in comet which passed Gamma Hydra Four. Said comet is now——" He looked at Spock.

"Quadrant four four eight, sir."

"I suggest all units be alerted for complete analysis of radiation; and means found to neutralize it. The comet is highly dangerous. Kirk, commanding *Enterprise*. Send it at once, Lieutenant Uhura. Let's go, Mr. Spock."

At the elevator he paused. "Mr. Sulu, increase orbit to twenty thousand miles perigee."

Startled, Sulu said, "You mean—another twenty thousand, Captain?"

Kirk whipped around, grim-faced. "I find it difficult to understand why every one of my commands is being questioned. Do what you're told, Mr. Sulu."

Spock spoke quietly. "What is our present position, Mr. Sulu?"

"Orbiting at twenty thousand, sir."

Kirk looked at Spock's impassive face. Then he said, "Maintain, Mr. Sulu."

"Maintaining, sir."

The silence of constraint was heavy in the bridge when the elevator door closed behind them.

But in Sickbay, hope had returned.

"Radiation," McCoy said reflectively. "As good an answer as any. But why didn't we know this earlier?"

"I suspect, Doctor, because my thinking processes are less clear and rapid than they were."

McCoy glanced at Spock. Then he handed his tape cartridge to Janet Wallace. "Run this through, please, Doctor."

110

"All right," Kirk said. "Keep me posted. I'll be on the bridge. Coming, Spock?"

"I have a question for the Doctor, Captain."

Kirk nodded, left. Spock said, "Doctor, the ship's temperature is increasingly uncomfortable for me. I have adjusted the environment in my quarters to one hundred and twenty-five degrees. This at least is tolerable, but—"

"I can see I won't be making any house calls on you," McCoy said.

"I wondered if there was something which could lower my sensitivity to cold."

"I'm not a magician, Spock. Just a plain old country doctor."

As the Vulcan closed the Sickbay door behind him, Janet turned, frustrated, from the computer. "Dr. McCoy, none of our usual radiation therapies will have any effect on this particular form of radiation sickness."

"All right. We start over. We work harder. Faster. Start completely from scratch if we have to. But we must find something."

Outside in the corridor, Commodore Stocker had intercepted Spock. "Can I have a word with you, Mr. Spock?"

"Commodore?"

Stocker lowered his voice. "Mr. Spock, a Starship can function with a chief engineer, a chief medical officer, even a First Officer who is under physical par. But it is disastrous to have a commanding officer whose condition is less than perfection."

"I am aware of that."

"Please understand me. My admiration for Captain Kirk is unbounded. He is a great officer. But . . . Mr. Spock, I need your help and your cooperation."

"For what, sir?"

"I want you to take over command of the *Enterprise*."

"On what grounds, sir?"

"On the grounds that the Captain is unable to perform his duties because of his affliction."

"I must remind you that I have contracted the same affliction."

"But you're a Vulcan," Stocker said. "You have a

much greater life span. You show the effects to a much smaller degree . . ."

"I am half human, sir," Spock said. "My physical reflexes are down. My mental capacities are reduced. I tire easily. No, sir. I am not fit for command."

"If you, a Vulcan, are not, then obviously Captain Kirk cannot be."

"Sir," Spock said, "I have duties to perform."

"Mr. Spock, I do not like what I'm about to say but regulations demand it. As second in command of the *Enterprise,* you must convene an extraordinary hearing on the Captain's competence."

"I—resist that suggestion, sir," Spock said stiffly.

"It's not a matter of choice. If a Captain is mentally or physically unfit, a competency hearing is mandatory. Please don't force me to quote a regulation which you know as well as I do."

There was a long pause. "Very well," Spock said. "The hearing will convene at fourteen hundred hours."

Under the eyes of a worried Kirk, Janet and McCoy were running final tests of Chekov. The unhappy Ensign was obviously considering rebellion against what seemed to be the thousandth needle jabbed into him during the course of these interminable examinations.

"Now, this won't hurt," McCoy told him.

"That's what you said last time," Chekov said. "And the time before that."

"Did it hurt?"

"Yes," Chekov retorted.

From the door of Sickbay came a whimper: "Doctor . . . help me . . ."

They turned. Arlene Galway was clutching the doorjamb for support. She was almost unrecognizable with age. "Please . . . do something . . . help . . ."

She reached out a hand; but before anyone could reach her, she collapsed to the deck. McCoy bent over her, while Kirk looked on, appalled even through the gray fog in which everything seemed to have happened in the last few days—or was it the last few weeks?

"That can't be—Lieutenant Galway?" he quavered.

"It is," McCoy said, his own voice creaky. "Or was.

She's dead. Her higher metabolism rate caused her to age more rapidly than the rest of us. But it's only a question of time before—"

"Bones, how long have we got?"

"Oh, it's a matter of days, Jim . . . perhaps only hours."

It wasn't information calculated to tranquilize a Starfleet captain called to a hearing on his command competence. Nor were the people gathered around the briefing-room table a quieting influence. The mysterious radiation sickness had made deeper inroads on everyone who had made the ill-fated check on the Robert Johnson expedition.

Looking as though he'd passed his fiftieth birthday, Spock opened the hearing by turning to Yeoman Atkins, who was serving as recorder. "Let it be read that this competency hearing has been ordered by Commodore Stocker, here present." He paused. "And reluctantly called by myself."

Kirk said, "Let it also be read that I consider this hearing invalid."

Spock looked down the table at Stocker.

Stocker said, "Regulation seven five nine two, section three paragraph eleven . . ."

"I know the book, Commodore," Kirk said.

Spock said quietly, "The legality of the hearing, Captain, is unquestionable."

"Mr. Spock, may I make a statement?" It was Stocker's question. At Spock's nod, he said, "I've had to resort to these legal grounds to save the lives of some extremely valuable members of the Starfleet. I have tried to convince Captain Kirk of the need to proceed to Star Base Ten—but have been overruled in each case. The responsibility for this hearing is mine."

"On the contrary, Commodore," Spock said. "As presiding officer and second in command of the *Enterprise,* the responsibility is mine. Captain Kirk, would you like to make a statement?"

"Yes!" The word came in a shout. "I am Captain of this ship and am totally capable of commanding her. Call this farce off and let's get back to work!"

"I cannot, sir," Spock said. "The regulations are quite specific." The chill struck him again. "You are entitled, sir, to direct examination of all witnesses immediately after this board has questioned them."

Kirk's voice was acid with sarcasm. "That is very kind of you, Mr. Spock."

Spock pushed a button on the computer-recorder. Imperturbable, he said, "Mr. Sulu, how long have you served with Captain Kirk?"

"Two years, sir."

"To your knowledge has he ever been unable to make decisions?"

"No, sir."

"Did he order you to maintain standard orbit around Gamma Hydra Four?"

"Yes, sir."

"Did he, several minutes later, repeat the order?"

"Yes, sir."

"Did he order you to increase orbit to twenty thousand perigee?"

"Yes, sir."

"And did he not repeat that order?"

"He did not!" Kirk yelled. "When I give an order I expect it to be obeyed! I don't have to repeat myself!"

"Captain, you'll be allowed direct cross-examination privileges when the board has finished."

"Isn't your terminology mixed up, Spock? This isn't a board! It's a cudgel!"

"Captain, it is a hearing not only sanctioned but required by regulations. Will you please answer the question, Mr. Sulu?"

"Yes, sir. Captain Kirk repeated his order."

"Commodore?"

"I have no questions," Stocker said.

"Captain Kirk?"

"Let's get on with it."

Spock ground his teeth together to keep them from chattering. His hands felt clumsy with cold. "Yeoman Atkins, you handed Captain Kirk a fuel-consumption report before witnesses. He accepted and signed it. Is that correct?"

"Sir, he had more important things on his mind. The current crisis—"

"Yeoman, you are merely to answer the question."

"I—guess he forgot he'd signed it."

"You guess?"

"He forgot he'd signed it."

"Thank you, Yeoman. You may leave."

It went on. Spock called Uhura to testify to Kirk's failure to recall that the Romulans had broken Code Two.

"All right!" Kirk cried. "I had a lot on my mind! I admit to the oversight!"

"It could have been a dangerous one," Stocker said.

"You are out of order, Commodore," Spock said. "Dr. McCoy?"

McCoy was lost in a daydream. "Dr. McCoy!"

He roused. "Sorry. Yes, Mr. Spock?"

"Several hours ago, at this board's request, you ran a complete physical examination of Captain Kirk."

"I did." McCoy threw a tape across the table at Spock. "It's all there. Enjoy yourself."

Silently, the Vulcan placed the tape cartridge into the computer slot.

The device buzzed, clicked, spoke. "Subject's physical age, based on physiological profile, sixty-three solar years."

There was a silence. Then Kirk said, "I am thirty-four years old."

"The computer differs with you," Stocker said.

"Dr. McCoy, give us your professional evaluation of Captain Kirk's present physical condition."

McCoy averted his eyes from Spock. "He is afflicted with a strange type of radiation sickness . . . and so are you and I and Mr. Scott."

"Kindly restrict your comments to Captain Kirk alone, Doctor. What effect has this sickness had on him?"

"He's—he's graying a little. A touch of arthritis."

"Is that all?"

"You know it isn't all! What are trying to do, Spock?"

"What I must do. Is not the Captain suffering from

115

a peculiar physical degeneration which strongly resembles aging?"

"Yes, he is. But he's a better man—"

"Doctor, do you agree with the computer's evaluation of the Captain's physical age?"

"It's a blasted machine!"

"Do you agree with it, Doctor?"

"Yes, I agree. I'm sorry, Jim."

"This board has no further questions. Unless you, Commodore Stocker . . ."

"I am quite satisfied, Mr. Spock."

"Do you wish to call witnesses, Captain Kirk?"

"I am perfectly capable of speaking in my own defense!"

Kirk tried to rise. His knee gave way; and he clutched at the table to keep from falling. "This hearing is being held for one reason and one alone. Because I refuse to leave Gamma Hydra Two."

"Gamma Hydra Four, sir," Spock said.

"Of course. A slip of the tongue. Where was I?" He suddenly clenched his fist and dashed it against the table. "So I'm a little confused! Who wouldn't be at a time like this? My ship in trouble . . . my senior officers ill . . . and this—this nonsense about a competency hearing! Enough to mix up any man! Trying to relieve a Starfleet captain of his command. Why, that's . . . that's . . . I wouldn't have believed it of you, Spock!"

He glared around the table. "All right, ask me questions! Go ahead! I'll show you who's capable! There's nothing wrong with my memory. Nor with my resolution, either. I repeat, we are maintaining orbit around Gamma Hydra Two!"

The second memory failure stood out, stark-naked.

Spock, cold to his marrow, spoke quietly into the silence.

"We have no more questions, Captain." He struggled to control his shivering. "If you will leave the room, sir, while the board votes . . ."

"Fine! You bet I'll leave it. Get your stupid voting over so I can get back to running my ship!"

He limped to the door and turned. "If I'm wanted, I'll be in my quarters."

When the door closed behind him, Spock said, "A simple hand vote will suffice. Dr. Wallace is excluded from the vote. Those who agree that Captain Kirk is no longer capable of handling the *Enterprise* will so signify by raising their right hands."

All hands save Spock's were slowly raised.

"Mr. Spock?" It was Commodore Stocker.

Spock raised his hand. He addressed the recording computer. "Register a unanimous vote."

Stocker said, "I assume, Mr. Spock, that you will now take over command of this vessel."

"Your assumption is incorrect, sir."

"Your reason?"

"By the standards this hearing has used against the Captain: my own physical failings exclude me from any command position."

"All right. Next in line is Mr. Scott."

All eyes fixed on Scott. He peered at the expectant faces, blinked, nodded—and was asleep.

"Since all senior officers are incapable, I am forced by regulations to assume command." Stocker was rising from the table when Spock said, "Sir, you have never commanded a starship."

"Whom would you have take over, Mr. Spock?"

"There is danger from the Romulans," Spock said.

"Mr. Spock, we've got to save these people!" He turned to Sulu. "Mr. Sulu, lay a direct course for Star Base Ten. Warp Five."

"Across the neutral zone, sir?"

Stocker nodded. "Alter course immediately."

"Commodore Stocker, I beg you not to underestimate the danger. Or the Romulans." Spock spoke urgently.

"The neutral zone is thinly patrolled at best. I am gambling that the violation will escape the Romulans' notice."

"The gamble, sir, if I may quote the odds—" Spock said.

"You may not!" Stocker strode to the door. "All officers are to return to their stations."

Kirk was alone in his quarters, tired, defeated, crushed by the full weight of his seventy years. When the knock at the door came, he could hardly bring himself to respond to it; but after a moment, he said, "Come in."

Spock entered, followed by Janet, who took up an inconspicuous stance beside the door. Kirk looked up hopefully at Spock, but the First Officer's face, for once, was almost as readable as a book.

"So," Kirk said. "I've been relieved."

"I am sorry, Captain."

"You should have been a prosecuting attorney."

"Regulations required me——"

"Regulations!" Kirk said. "Don't give me regulations, Spock! You've wanted command all along! The first little excuse——"

"I have not assumed command, Captain."

"I hope you're proud of the way you got . . ." Kirk paused, Spock's words gradually coming home. "What do you mean, you're not in command?"

"I suffer from the same ailment as yourself, sir."

"If you're not in command, who is?"

"Commodore Stocker."

It took Kirk a long moment to place the name. Then he exploded. "Stocker? Are you crazy? He's never held a field command! If Scotty——"

"Mr. Scott is in no condition to command. Commodore Stocker, as a ranking officer——"

"Don't prate to me about rank. The man's a chairbound paper-pusher. Spock, I order you to take command!"

"I cannot, sir."

"You are disobeying a direct order, Mr. Spock."

"No, Captain. Only Commodore Stocker can give command orders on this ship now."

Impotent fury rose in Kirk. "You disloyal, traitorous . . . you stabbed me in the back the first chance you had. You——" His rage mounted as he found that he was weeping. Weeping! "Get out of here! I don't ever want to have to look at you again!"

Spock hesitated, inclined his head slightly, and left. After a moment, Kirk became aware of the female figure still standing beside the door inside his room, making faint sniffling noises. He peered at it.

"Who is it? Jan? Jan?"

"I'm sorry, Jim," she said. "Truly I am."

"I acted like a fool in there. Let them rattle me. Let myself get confused."

"Everyone understood."

"Only I'm not old, Jan. I'm not! A few muscular aches don't make a man old! You don't run a starship with your arms—you run it with your head! My mind's as sharp as it ever was!"

"We'll find a cure."

"A simple case of radiation sickness and I'm relieved of command." He turned and looked at himself in a mirror. "All right, I admit I've gotten a little gray. Radiation can do that."

"Jim," she said, as if in pain. "I have work to do. Please excuse me—"

"Look at me, Jan. You said you loved me. You know me. Look closely—"

"Please, Jim—"

"Just need a little rest. That's all. I'm not old, am I? Well, Say it! Say I'm not old!"

There was no response. Grasping her by the shoulders, he pulled her to him and kissed her with all the violence of which he was capable. But there was no response—not from her, and what was worse, not even within himself. He released her—and saw the pity in her eyes. He turned his back.

"Get out."

Now what? He could not think. He was relieved. The answer . . . but there was no answer. Wait. Something about a comet. McCoy. Chekov. The examination room. That was it, the examination room. He hobbled out, cursing himself for his slowness.

Spock was there; so were Nurse Chapel, McCoy and Janet. They all looked very old, somehow. But the hapless Chekov, back on the table again, did not seem to have changed. He was saying: "Why don't I just go back to work and leave my blood here?"

Kirk tried to glare at Spock. "What are you doing here?"

"It would seem the place where I can be of the most use."

"Maybe you'd like to relieve Dr. McCoy? Bones, what about Ensign Chekov here?"

"Nothing," McCoy said peevishly. "Absolutely nothing."

"There has to be! There has to be! We went down to the surface together. Beamed-down together. Stayed in the same spot. He was with us all the time. He—"

"*No,* Captain," Spock said, drawing in a sharp breath. "Not all the time. He left us for a few moments."

"Left us?" Kirk stared at the Vulcan, trying to remember. "Oh. Yes—when he went into the building. He . . . there was . . . Spock! Something did happen!"

"Indeed, Captain. Doctor, you will remember Professor Alvin's corpse in the improvised coffin—"

"Chekov, you got scared!" Kirk crowed. "You bumped into the dead man, and—"

"You bet," Chekov said. "I was scared, sir. But not half as scared as I am now, I'll tell you that."

"Fright?" McCoy said, raising a trembling hand to his chin. "Yes. Could be. Heart beats faster. Breath short. Cold sweat. Epinephrine flows. Something I read once . . . epinephrine tried for radiation sickness, in the mid-twentieth century—"

"It was abandoned," Janet said. "When hyronalyn was discovered."

"Yes, yes," McCoy said testily. "Don't confuse me. Why was it abandoned? There was some other reason. I knew it well, once. They didn't know the intermediate? Yes! That's it! AMP! Nurse, ask the computer for something called AMP!"

Christine Chapel, her face a study in incredulitity, turned to the computer read-out panel. After what seemed a very long time, she said, "There's an entry for it. It's called cyclic adenosine three-five monophosphate. But it affects *all* the hormonal processes—that's why they dropped it."

"We'll try it," McCoy said, with a startling cackle. "Don't just stand there, Dr. Wallace. Synthesize me a batch. Dammit, get cracking!"

On the bridge, Commodore Stocker was in the command chair. If he was aware of how many backs were pointedly turned to him, he did not show it; he was too busy trying to make sense of the many little lights that were flickering across the console before him.

"Entering Romulan neutral zone, sir," the helmsman said. "All sensors on maximum."

Now who was that? "Thank you, Mr. Spock, sorry, Mr. Sulu. Lieutenant Uhura, let me know if we contact any Romulan."

"Yes, sir. Nothing yet."

Stocker nodded and looked down again. The little lights danced mockingly at him. As a cadet he had studied a control board something like this, but since then, everything seemed to have been rearranged, and labeled with new symbols which meant nothing to him, with only a few exceptions. Well, he would have to depend upon these officers—

Then the *Enterprise* shook sharply under him, and half of the little lights went red. Ignorance overwhelmed him. "What was that?" he said helplessly.

"We have made contact, sir," Uhura said in a dry voice.

"Romulans approach from both sides, sir," Sulu added.

The ship shook again, harder. Swallowing, Stocker said, "Let's see them."

The main viewscreen lit up. It too was full of crawling little lights, which could not be told from the stars except for their motions, which he could not read either.

"I don't see any Romulans!"

"The ones that are changing color, sir. They change in accordance with their rate of approach—"

The ship bucked under him. All the lights went red.

"We're bracketed, sir," Sulu said evenly.

There was a buzz he couldn't locate. "Engineering calling, sir," Uhura said. "Do you want power diverted to the shields?"

His face felt bathed in sweat. "Yes," he said, at random.

"Mr. Scott asks how much warp power to reserve."

What was the answer to that one?

"Commodore Stocker," Sulu said, turning halfway toward the command chair. "We're in a tight. What are your orders?"

The *Enterprise* shuddered once more, and the lights dimmed. Stocker realized suddenly that he was too scared to speak, let alone move—

Then, mercifully, Kirk's voice, thin but demanding, came through the intercom. "What's going on up there? Lieutenant Uhura, this is the Captain!"

"Sir!" Uhura said. "We have violated the Romulan neutral zone, and are under attack."

"The fool. Maintain full shields! I'll be right there."

Stocker felt as though he were about to pass out with relief, but the ordeal wasn't over yet. Voices, more distant, were arguing over the open intercom:

"Jim . . . you can't . . . neither of us . . . Nurse . . . Doctor Wallace . . ."

"Got to . . . get to the bridge . . ."

"Oh Jim, you can't . . . Nurse . . . In there . . ."

Then the voices snapped off. Clearly, Kirk was not about to bail Stocker out yet. Rousing himself, Stocker said, "Lieutenant Uhura, keep trying to raise the Romulans."

"Very well. No response thus far."

"If I can talk to them—tell them the reason why we've violated the neutral zone—"

"The Romulans are notorious for not listening to explanations," Sulu said. "We know—we've tangled with them before."

"Hail them again!"

"I've hailed them on all channels," Uhura said. "They're ignoring us."

"Why shouldn't they?" Sulu said. "They know they have us. As long as we sit here, they can kick away at the screens until they go down."

Stocker ran a hand through his hair. "Then," he said, "we have no alternative but to surrender."

"They'd love that," Sulu said, his back still turned. "They have never captured a starship before. And, Commodore, they never take prisoners."

"Then what—"

"Sir," Uhura said, "you are in command. *What are your orders?*"

In Sickbay, Nurse Chapel and Janet had Kirk pinned down on a bed. He struggled to get up, and despite his aged condition they were having trouble restraining him—a task further complicated by the unpredictable shuddering of the *Enterprise.*

"Greenhorn—up there—ruin my ship—"

"Jim," Janet said through gritted teeth, "if I have to give you a shot—"

"Jim, lay quiet," McCoy said. "You can't do any good. We're through."

"No, no. My ship—"

Spock appeared from the laboratory, carrying a flask. "Dr. Wallace, here is the drug. It's crude, but we had no time for pharmacological tests or other refinements."

"All right," said McCoy. "Let's go."

"It will cure . . . or kill." Spock handed the flask to Janet, who loaded a hypo from it. "A safer preparation would take weeks to test."

"What is it?" Kirk said, quietening somewhat.

"The hormone intermediate," Janet said. "It has to be given parenterally, and even without the probable impurities in it, it could be extremely hard on the body. Cerebral hemmorhage, cardiac arrest—"

"Never mind the details," McCoy said. "Give it to me."

"No," Kirk said. "I'll take the first shot."

"You can't," McCoy said firmly.

As if on cue, the *Enterprise* shook again. "How long do you think the ship can take a pounding like this?" Kirk demanded. "I've got to get up there!"

"Jim, this could kill you," Janet said.

"I'll die anyway without it."

"Medical ethics demand—" McCoy began.

"Forget medical ethics! My ship is being destroyed! Give me that shot."

"The Captain is correct," Spock said. "If he does not regain his faculties, and get to the bridge to take command in a very few minutes, we shall all die at

123

the hands of the Romulans. Give him the shot, Dr. Wallace."

She did so. For a moment nothing seemed to happen. Then Kirk found himself in the throes of convulsions, bucking and flailing at random. Dimly he was aware that all four of the others were hanging on to him.

It seemed to last forever, but actually hardly a minute passed before the fit began to subside, to be gradually replaced by a feeling of exhausted well-being. Janet was pointing a Feinberger at him.

"It's working," she said in a hushed voice. "The aging process has stopped."

"Can't see any change," McCoy said.

"She is correct, Doctor," Spock said. "It is there, and accelerating."

"Janet, help me up," Kirk said, taking a deep breath. "That was quite a ride."

"How do you feel?" she said.

"Like I've been kicked through the bulkhead. Spock, you'll have to wait for your shot; I need you on the bridge. Janet, give McCoy his shot, then Scott." He smiled. "Besides, Spock—if what I've got in mind doesn't work, you won't need that shot. Let's go."

In transit, he felt stronger and more acute with every passing second, and judging by the looks of relief with which he was greeted on the bridge, the change was visible to others as well.

"Report, Sulu!"

"We are surrounded by Romulan vessels—maximum of ten. Range, fifty to a hundred thousand kilometers."

Stocker got out of the command chair in a hurry as Kirk approached it. Kirk punched the intercom. "Engineering, feed in all emergency power, and all warp-drive engines on full standby. I'm going to need the works in about two minutes. Captain out . . . Lieutenant Uhura, set up a special channel to Starfleet Command. Code Two."

"But, Captain—"

"I gave you an order, Lieutenant. Code Two."

"Code Two, sir."

"Message: *Enterprise* to Starfleet Command, this

sector. Ship has inadvertantly encroached upon Romulan neutral zone. Surrounded and under heavy Romulan attack. Escape impossible. Shields failing. Will implement destruct order, using corbomite device recently installed. Since this will result in destruction of *Enterprise* and all matter within two hundred thousand kilometer diameter, and establish corresponding dead zone, all Federation ships to avoid area for at least four solar years. Explosion will occur in one minute. Kirk, commanding *Enterprise*. Out . . . Mr. Sulu. Course 188, mark 14, Warp Eight and stand by."

"Standing by, sir."

From his station, Spock said, "The Romulans are giving ground, sir. I believe they tapped in, as you obviously expected them to."

"A logical assumption, Mr. Spock. Are they still retreating?"

"Yes, sir, but are still well within firing range."

"All hands stand by . . . now, Warp Eight!"

The ship jolted—not this time to an onslaught, but to sudden motion at eight times the speed of light. Spock hovered over his console.

"The Romulans were caught off guard, sir. Not even in motion yet."

"Are we out of range, Mr. Sulu?"

"Yes, sir. And out of the neutral zone."

"Adjust to new course. One nine two degrees, mark 4. Heading for Star Base Ten."

"Coming around, sir."

Kirk sat back. He felt fine. Commodore Stocker approached him, his face full of shame.

"Captain," Stocker said, "I just wanted to assure you that I did what I thought had to be done to save you and the other officers."

"Noted, Commodore. You should know, however, that there is very little a Star Base can do that a starship cannot."

"If I may say so, Captain, I am now quite aware of what a starship can do—with the right man at the helm."

The elevator doors snapped open and McCoy came out. He was as young as ever. Kirk stared at him.

"You're looking good, Bones."

"So's Scotty. The drug worked. He pulled a muscle during the initial reaction, but otherwise he's feeling fine. Now, Mr. Spock, whenever you're ready."

"I'm ready now, Doctor."

"Good. Because of your Vulcan physique, I've prepared an extremely potent shot. I've also removed all the breakables from Sickbay."

"That is very thoughtful of you."

"I knew you'd appreciate it."

Kirk smiled. "All in all, gentlemen, an experience we'll remember in our old age . . . of course, that won't be for a long time yet, will it?"

ELAAN OF TROYIUS

(John Meredyth Lucas)

Kirk's orders were simple. He was to "cooperate" in all matters pertaining to the mission of his passenger, the Ambassador of the planet Troyius.

It was the implications of his orders that were complicated. First, the Ambassador's mission was top secret. Second, his negotiations involved the notoriously hostile people of Elas, a neighbor planet. As if such "cooperation" weren't enough of a headache, both planets were located in a star system over which the Klingon Empire claimed jurisdiction. By entering the system, the *Enterprise* was inviting Klingon retaliation for trespass.

Kirk was frankly irritated as he swung his command chair to Uhura. "Inform Transporter Room we'll be beaming-up the Elas party at once. Ask Ambassador Petri to meet us there."

"Yes, Captain."

At his nod, Spock, McCoy and Scott followed him into the elevator. Kirk said, "Some deskbound Starfleet bureaucrat has cut these cloak-and-dagger orders."

The intercom spoke. "Bridge to Captain." It was Uhura's voice.

"Kirk here."

127

"Captain, signal from the Elas party. They're ready to beam aboard but demand an explanation of the delay."

"Here we go," Kirk said. "What delay are they talking about? All right. Forget it, Lieutenant Uhura. Beam them aboard."

Spock said, "The attitude is typical of the Elasians, sir. Scientists who made the original survey of the planet described their men as vicious and arrogant."

"That's the negative aspect," McCoy said. "I've gone over those records. Their women are supposed to be something very special. They're said to possess a kind of subtle—maybe mystical—power that drives men wild."

Spock gave McCoy a disgusted look. It was still on his face when the elevator door opened to reveal the waiting Troyian envoy. Kirk addressed him immediately. "Ambassador Petri, suppose you drop this diplomatic secrecy—and tell me what this mission of yours is really about."

"That must wait until the Dohlman of Elas is aboard, Captain."

"Dohlman?" Kirk said as they all entered the Transporter Room. "What the devil is a Dohlman?"

"The thing most feared and hated by my people. Our most deadly enemy," Petri said.

The Transporter Room's hum deepened—and three figures sparkled into substance on the platform. They were soldiers. Breast plates covered their chests. Weapons of no recognizable variety hung from the barbaric chains around their necks. The biggest Elasian soldier, thick-jawed, heavy-browed, covered the *Enterprise* group with his strange weapon.

"Welcome. I am the Ambassador of Troyius," Petri said.

The ape-jawed giant ignored him. "Who runs this ship?"

Kirk said, "The *Enterprise* is under my command. I am Captain Kirk."

"And I am Kryton of Elas. That Troyian there is a menace. I must know that all is secure here before the Dohlman is brought aboard."

Spock lowered his voice. "Captain, the weapons resemble twenty-first century nuclear disintegrators."

Kirk spoke to the bellicose Kryton. "My ship *is* secure. What's more, we are equipped to repel any hostile act." He turned his back on the Elasian to say to the Transporter Room technician. "Energize!"

The center transporter platform went luminous. The three Elasians dropped to one knee. Glaring at Kirk, Kryton growled, "Quickly! To your knee! Do honor to the Dohlman of Elas!"

Kirk's jaw tightened. Beside him, acquiescent, Petri sank to one knee. "It is their custom," he muttered. "To stand is a breach of protocol."

Spock looked at Kirk. Annoyance on his face, Kirk nodded. The Vulcan hesitated; then, he, too, bent his knee. The sight increased Kirk's annoyance. It was abruptly dissipated. On the center platform the "deadly enemy" of Troyius had appeared. The Dohlman was a silver blonde. Her skin had the pearly tone of dreams. So was her body the stuff of dreams. Nor was it hidden. The scanty metallic scarves she wore served no purpose but suggestion of beauty too overwhelming for complete revelation.

Kryton said, "Glory to Elaan, Dohlman of Elas!"

"Glory is right," Kirk thought, controlling an impulse to kneel himself. Instead, he bowed. Then, raising his head, he looked again at the Dohlman of Elas. Under the silver blonde hair, her eyes were dark. Aflame with contempt, they swept over the kneeling men. At a snap of her fingers, her soldier bodyguard got to their feet, Kryton, addressing Spock and Petri, said, "Now you may stand."

She came forward, Kryton towering behind her, tense, his weapon at the ready. Her own hand rested on the elaborately jeweled hilt of a dagger suspended from a golden chain she wore around her slim waist.

"Odd," Kirk said to Spock. "Body armor and nuclear weapons."

"Not without precedent, sir. Consider the Samurai customs of old Earth's Japanese. Even we Vulcans preserve some symbolic remnants of our past."

Kryton growled again. "Permission to speak was not given!"

Before Kirk could retort, Elaan said to Spock, "You rule this ship?" The voice was husky, infinitely feminine.

"I am the ship's First Officer. This is Captain Kirk."

She made no sign of acknowledgment. Petri interposed hastily. "Your glory, I am Petri of Troyius. In the name of my people, I bid you welcome to——"

"Your mission is known to me," she said with negligent scorn. Then, turning to Kirk, she added, "You are permitted to show the accommodations."

He pulled himself together. "I think we'd better have an understanding right——"

"Please, Captain," Petri begged.

Kirk said, "My First Officer, Mr. Spock will show you to your quarters." He turned to leave. "Ambassador Petri, I want to speak to you."

Elaan's words came like a whip. "You have not been dismissed."

Incredulous, on the edge of explosion, Kirk gave his response second thought. He decided to shrug. "May I have your glory's permission to leave?" he asked silkily.

"You are all dismissed," she said.

Outside in the corridor Kirk wheeled on Petri. "All right, Ambassador! What exactly are we supposed to be doing?"

Petri drew him aside. "She—that woman is to be the wife of our ruler. The marriage has been arranged to bring peace. Our two warring planets now possess the capability of mutual destruction. Some method of coexistence had to be found."

"Then we return to Troyius?"

"Yes. But slowly, Captain. I will need time. My mission is to teach her civilized manners before we reach Troyius. It must be clear to you now why I'll need time. In her present savage condition my people would never accept her as queen."

"You've got yourself quite a mission," Kirk said.

"Those are my orders. I must ask you and your crew to tolerate this Elasian impudence for the sake

130

of future peace. It is vital that friction now be kept to a minimum."

"That I can understand," Kirk said.

"There's another thing you should understand, Captain. You have as much at stake as I have. Your superiors know that failure of this mission would be as catastrophic for Federation planning as it would be for our two planets. The peace we'd gain by accepting such an untutored wife for our ruler would not be peace." He drew a deep sighing breath. "I will take her the official gifts I bear. Perhaps they will change her mood."

Kirk said, "I hope so." But what he thought was: "Shrew, termagant—a knockout fishwife is what I've got on my ship!"

Troubled, he stopped at Sulu's station as he re-entered the bridge. "Mr. Sulu, lay in a course for Troyius. Impulse drive-speed factor point zero three seven. Take us out of orbit."

Sulu looked startled. "Impulse drive, Captain?"

"That is correct, Mr. Sulu. Sub-light factor point zero three seven."

Scott looked up from his station. "Captain, you'll not be using the warp drive? All the way on impulse?"

"Correct, Mr. Scott."

"That'll take a great deal of time."

"Are you in a hurry, Mr. Scott?"

"No, sir."

"That's it, then." But he'd scarcely reached his command chair when Spock hurried to his side. "Captain, the Dohlman is dissatisfied with her quarters!"

Overhearing, Uhura turned indignantly. "What's the matter with them?"

"Nothing that I was able to see," Spock said. "But all the Elasians seem to be most irrational."

"I gave up my quarters," Uhura said, "because—"

"*I* appreciate your sacrifice, Lieutenant," Kirk told her. He got up. "I'll talk to the lady myself."

He heard the screams of rage before he reached Uhura's cabin. Its door was wide open. But it took a moment to take in the scene. A crystal box was flying through the air—and struck Petri in the chest. "Swine!

131

Take back your gifts! Your ruler cannot buy the favor of the Dohlman of Elas!"

Petri retrieved the box, stuffing delicate lace back into it. "Your glory," he said, "this is your wedding veil." He backed up to what he clearly hoped was a safe distance to raise the lid of a begemmed gold casket. "In this," he said, "are the most prized royal jewels of Troyius. This necklace is a gift from the bridegroom's mother to adorn your lovely throat . . ."

The necklace seemed to be composed of diamonds and emeralds. Elaan seized it. Then she hurled it at Petri with a wild aim that barely escaped hitting Kirk in the face. "I would strangle if I wore this bauble of Troyian dogs around my neck!"

Kirk stepped over the glitter at his feet and into the cabin. She saw him and shrieked, "Kryton!" The huge guard rushed in. "By whose permission has *he* come here?"

"He came in answer to your summons, your glory."

Kirk said, "I understand you are not happy with your quarters."

She waved a hand, dismissing Kryton. "Quarters?" She leveled a perfect leg at a cushioned chair. "Am I a soft, pewling Troyian that I must have cushions to sit on?" She kicked the chair over. Her own action inflamed her rage. She ran to the cabin window, ripping down its draperies. "These female trappings in here are an offense to me!"

Kirk said, "My Communications Officer vacated these rooms in the generous hope you would find them satisfactory."

"I do not find them so." She pointed at Petri. "And I find this—this Ambassador even less satisfactory! Must my bitterness be compounded by his presence aboard your ship?"

Petri, red with suppressed fury, said, "I've explained to her glory that her Council of Nobles and the Troyian Tribunal jointly agreed that I should instruct—make her acquainted with the customs and manners of our people."

"Kryton!" Elaan called. She indicated Petri. "Remove him!" The guard fingered his weapon. Petri

132

bowed; and was moving to the door when she cried, "And take that garbage with you!" He bowed again, stooped lower to collect the gifts she'd flung to the floor and gratefully made his exit.

"That he should dare to suggest I adopt the servile manners of his people!" Elaan stormed.

"Your glory doesn't seem to be responding favorably to Troyian instruction," Kirk said.

"I will never forgive the Council of Nobles for inflicting such a nightmare on me! By the way, *you* were responding to my demand for better quarters!"

"There are none better aboard," Kirk said. "I suggest you make the best of it."

Aghast at this effrontery, she glanced at Uhura's dressing table for some object she could smash. "You presume to suggest to *me*——"

Kirk said, "Lieutenant Uhura's personal belongings have all been removed from the cabin. But if smashing things gratifies you, I will arrange to equip it with breakable articles."

"I will not be humiliated!"

"Then behave yourself," Kirk said. He went to the door; and she screamed, "I did not give you permission to leave!"

"I didn't ask for it," he said, slamming the door behind him.

An agitated Petri was waiting for him in the corridor. "Captain, I wish to contact my government. I cannot fulfill my mission. I would be an insult to my ruler to bring him this incorrigible monster as a bride."

"Simmer down, Ambassador. Your mission is a peace mission."

"There cannot be peace between the Elasians and us. We have deluded ourselves. The truth is, when I am with these people, I do not want peace. I want to kill them."

"Then you're as bad as she is," Kirk said. "You're not obliged to like the Elasians. You're obliged to do a job."

"The job's impossible. She simply won't listen to me."

"*Make* her listen," Kirk said. "Don't be so diplomatic. She respects strength. Come on strong with her, Ambassador."

"I, too, have pride, Captain. I will not be humiliated."

"You're on assignment, Ambassador. So am I. We're under orders to deliver the Dohlman in acceptable condition for this marriage. If it means swallowing a bit of our pride—well, that's part of the job."

Petri sighed. "Very well. I'll make another try."

"Strong, Ambassador. Remember, come on strong with her. Good luck."

A knockout fishwife. What she needed was a swift one to her lovely jaw. Kirk, re-entering the bridge was greeted by Uhura's hopeful question: "Does she like my quarters any better now, Captain?"

"She's made certain . . . arrangements, Lieutenant. But I think things will work out."

The intercom spoke excitedly. "Security alert! Deck five! Security alert!"

Kirk ran for the elevator. On deck five, Security Officer Evans met him as he stepped out. "It's Ambassador Petri, sir. They refuse to explain what happened but—"

At the door to Elaan's quarters, two *Enterprise* security men were confronting the three Elasian guards. "Stand aside, please," Kirk said to Kryton.

The ape-jawed giant said, "Her glory has not summoned you."

Behind him Elaan opened the closed door. "Have this Troyian pig removed," she said.

Petri lay on the cabin floor, face down in a pool of his own blood. The jeweled dagger had been buried in his back.

In Sickbay McCoy looked up at Kirk. "The knife went deep, Jim. He's lost a lot of blood."

Kirk bent over the patient. What he received was a glare. "If I recover," Petri said weakly, "it will be no thanks to you."

"I said talk to her. Not fight her."

"I should have known better than to enter that

cabin, unarmed. But you forced me to. I hold you responsible for this."

"Captain!" It was Uhura. "A message from Starfleet Command just in. Class A security, scrambled. I've just put it through the decoder."

"What is it, Lieutenant?"

"The Federation's High Commissioner is on his way to Troyius for the royal wedding."

McCoy whistled. "Whew! Now the fat's really in the fire. When the Commissioner learns the bride has just tried to murder the groom's Ambassador . . ."

"What a comfort you are, Bones!" But McCoy had returned to the patient whom Nurse Christine was preparing for an air hypo. As she applied it, she said, "If the Elasian women are this vicious, sir, why are men so attracted to them? What is their magic?"

"It's not magic," Petri said scornfully. "It's biochemical—a chemical substance in their tears. A man whose flesh is once touched by an Elasian woman's tears is made her slave forever."

"What rot!" Kirk thought. "The man's a fool." The failure of his mission was about to be exposed to the Federation's High Commissioner—and here he was going on about Elasian females' tears. He walked over to the bed. "Ambassador, I have news for you. The Federation's High Commissioner is on his way to this wedding."

"There will be no wedding. I would not have our ruler marry that creature if the entire galaxy depended on it. And I want nothing more to do with you."

"I didn't ask you to have anything to do with me. I asked you to do your job with her." He turned to McCoy. "Bones, how long will it take to get him back on his feet?"

"A few days. Maybe a week."

Petri raised his head from his pillow. "Captain, in this bed you put me. And in this bed I intend to stay. Indefinitely. I have nothing further to say to you."

Kirk looked at McCoy. Then he shrugged. Uhura and McCoy followed him out to the corridor. "I don't know what to do with him, Jim. He's as bad as she is. They're all pig-headed. And they just plain hate each other."

Uhura said, "You've got to admit he's got the better reason for hate. Captain, can't you explain to the High Commissioner that it's just impossible to—"

"High Commissioners don't like explanations. They like results. How do you handle a woman like that, anyway?"

"You stay away from her, Captain. As far away as—"

She broke off. From the recreation room they were passing came the sound of poignantly haunting music. Uhura's face lighted. "Captain, it used to be said that music hath charms to soothe the savage breast. The Dohlman has a very savage breast. Suppose you—"

"Soothing that woman is asking a lot of any music," McCoy said.

But Kirk was looking reflectively at the recreation room door. He opened it. Spock, sitting apart from the other crew members, was strumming his Vulcan lyre. Its unearthly tones suited the room decorations— its carpet of pink grass, wall vines that broke into drooping, long-stamened blossoms, the fountain spraying purple water into the air.

"Spock, what's that music you're playing?"

"A simple scale. I was just tuning the lyre."

"You can play tunes on that contraption?" McCoy said.

"I took second prize in the all-Vulcan music competition."

"Who took the first one?"

"My father."

"Can you play a love song?" Kirk said.

"A mating song. In ancient times the Vulcan lyre was used to stimulate the mating passion."

"We need some form of such stimulation on this ship," Kirk said. "A mating on Troyius is supposed to take place if we could just persuade the bride to participate in it."

"Inasmuch as she's just knifed her teacher in the bridegroom's etiquette, teaching it to her seems something of a baffler," McCoy said.

136

"Appoint another teacher," Spock said.

"You, Spock?"

"Certainly not. Logic dictates that the Dohlman will accept only the person of highest rank aboard this vessel."

Everybody looked at Kirk. He looked back at them, considering all the elements involved in Elaan's capitulation to reason.

"All right. Spock, give me five minutes and then start piping that music of yours into the Dohlman's quarters." He left; and as Spock's fingers moved over the strings of his instrument, Uhura sighed. "Mr. Spock, that music really gets to me."

"Yes, I also find it relaxing."

"Relaxing is the very last word I'd use to describe it," Uhura said. "I'd certainly like to learn how to play that lyre."

"I'd be glad to give you the theory, Lieutenant. However, to my knowledge no non-Vulcan has ever mastered the skill."

In Elaan's cabin Kirk was wishing he could give her the theory of acceptable table manners.

He watched her lift a wine bottle from her sumptuously spread dinner table, take a swig from it and wipe her mouth with a lovely arm. She swallowed, and replacing the bottle on the table, said, "So the Ambassador will recover. That's too bad." Then she grabbed a roasted squab from a plate. She bit a mouthful of breast meat from it; and tossing the rest of the delicacy over her shoulder, added, "You've delivered your message. You have my leave to go."

He was fascinated by the efficiency with which she managed to articulate and chew squab at the same time. "I'd like nothing better," he said. "But your glory's impetuous nature has—"

"That Troyian pig was in my quarters without permission. Naturally I stabbed him."

Kirk said, "You Elasians pride yourselves on being a warrior race. Then you must understand discipline—the ability to follow orders as well as to give them. You are under orders to marry the Troyian ruler and familiarize yourself with the habits of his people."

"Troyians disgust me," she said. "Any contact with them makes me feel soiled."

Her cheek was soiled by a large spot of grease from the squab. "It's my experience," Kirk said, "that the prejudices people feel disappear once they get to know each other."

Spock's music had begun to filter into the cabin. "That has not been my experience," she said, reaching for a rich cream pastry.

"In any case, we're still faced with a problem."

"Problem?"

"Your indoctrination in the customs of Troyius."

"I have eliminated that problem."

"No. You eliminated your teacher. The problem remains."

The luscious mouth smiled grimly. How, he couldn't figure out. "And its solution?" she said.

"A new teacher."

"Oh." She placed her dagger on the table. "What's that sickening sound?" The pastry in her hand, she rose, went to the intercom and switched off the Vulcan music. Licking cream from the pastry, she said, "And you—what can you teach me?"

"Table manners for one thing," he said.

He picked up a napkin, went to her, removed the pastry; and wiped her mouth, her cheek and fingers. "This," he said, "is a table napkin. Its function is to remove traces of the wine and food one has swallowed instead of leaving them on the mouth, the cheek, the fingers—and oh yes, the arm." He wiped her arm. Then, grasping it firmly, he led her over to the table.

"And this," he said, "is a plate. It holds food. It is specifically made to hold food, as floors are not. They are constructed to walk on." He poured wine into a glass; and held it up. "This is a glass," he said, "the vessel from which one drinks wine. A bottle, your glory, is merely intended to hold the wine."

She seized the bottle and took another swig from it. "Leave me," she said.

"You are going to learn what you've been ordered to learn," he said.

"You will return me to Elas at once!"

138

"That is impossible."

She stamped her foot. "What I command is always possible! I will not go to Troyius! I will not be given to a fat pig of a Troyian as a bride to stop a war!" She lifted the wine bottle again to her mouth. Kirk grabbed it.

"You enjoy the title of Dohlman," he said. "If you don't want the obligations that go with it, give it up!"

Her shock was genuine. "Nobody has ever dared to speak to me in such a manner!"

"That's your trouble," he said. "Nobody has ever told you the truth. You are an uncivilized little savage, a vicious, bad-tempered child in a woman's body . . ."

Her fist leaped out and connected with Kirk's jaw. She had pulled her arm back to strike him again when he grabbed it and slapped her as hard as he could across the face. The blow sent her sprawling back on the bed. Shaking with rage, Kirk shouted, "You've heard the truth from me for the first time in your spoiled life!"

He made for the door—and her dagger hissed past his ear to stick, quivering, in a wall plaque beside his head. He pulled it free; and tossing it back to her, said, "Tomorrow's lesson, your glory, will be on courtesy."

As he jerked the door closed behind him, she yanked wildly at the table cover. He didn't turn at the sound of crashing crockery.

He got out of the bridge elevator to see Spock absorbed in his sensor viewer. "Captain, look at this. At first I defined it as a sensor ghost. But I've run checks on all the instrumentation. The equipment is working perfectly."

Kirk examined the shadow. "Hydrogen cloud reflection?"

"None in the area. The ghost appears intermittently."

"Speculation, Mr. Spock?"

"None, sir. Insufficient data."

"It's not an instrument malfunction, not a reflection of natural phenomena. A space ship, then?"

The intercom beeped. Scott's voice was thick with anger.

"Captain, must I let these—these passengers fool

around with my equipment? I know what you said about showing them respect but . . ."

"Hang on, Scotty. And be pleasant no matter how it hurts. I'm on my way."

He was startled himself when he opened the door to Engineering. Elaan and her three guards had their heads bent over the warp-drive mechanism. Scott had somehow got his fury under control. He was saying, "I suppose, ma'am, that even our impulse drive must seem fast—"

"We are interested in how ships are used in combat, not in what drives them. Engines are for mechanics and other menials."

Scott choked. "Menials? How long do you think—"

"Mr. Scott!" Kirk said sharply.

He strode to Elaan. "Why didn't you tell me you wanted a tour of the engine room?"

"Do I not own the freedom of this ship? I have granted your men permission not to kneel in my presence. What more do you want?"

"Courtesy."

"Courtesy is not for inferiors."

Kirk said, "Mr. Scott, our chief engineer has received you into his department. That was a courtesy. You will respond to it by saying, 'Thank you, Mr. Scott.' "

He thought she was going to spit at him. Then she said tightly, "Thank you, Mr. Scott." Her guards stared, dumbfounded. She pushed one. "Come," she said to them and swept out.

Scott said, "Your schooling, sir, seems to be taking effect."

A buzz came from the intercom beside them. Spock's voice said, "Bridge to Captain."

"Kirk here."

"That sensor ghost is moving closer, sir."

"On my way."

His guess had been right. The sensor ghost was a space ship. Kirk studied the instrument for a long moment. Then he raised his head. "The question is, Mr. Spock, whose space ship is it?"

"No data yet, sir."

"Captain!" Sulu called. "A distant bearing, sir. Mark 73.5."

"Maximum magnification," Kirk said.

The main viewing screen had been merely showing a telescopic blur of a normally stationary star field. Now there suddenly swam into it the sharp image of an unfamiliar but strangely evil-looking space ship.

"Our ghost has materialized, Captain," Spock said. Kirk nodded soberly. "A Klingon warship."

He returned to his command chair, the gravity in his face deepened. He turned to look at the screen again. "Any change, Mr. Spock?"

"Negative, sir. The Klingon ship has simply moved into contact range. She's pacing us, precisely matching our sub-light speed."

Though the bridge screen was equipped to show what was moving outside the *Enterprise,* it was not equipped to show what was moving inside it. Thus, Kirk could not see Kryton move stealthily into the engineering room—and take cover behind the huge mount where Second Engineer Watson was working. In perfect secrecy, the Elasian silently removed the main relay box cover, took a small dial-studded disk from his uniform pouch, adjusted the dials and placed the disk in the relay box. It was as he fitted it that Watson sensed something amiss. Tool in hand, he confronted Kryton, shouting, "What are you doing in here?"

Kryton's fist came up under his chin like a uncoiled spring. Watson crumpled. In a flash, Kryton had the body hidden and huddled behind the mount. Then he went back to work in the relay box.

In the bridge, Kirk, still concentrated on the Klingon ship's doings, turned to Uhura. "Lieutenant, open a hailing frequency. Identify us and ask his intentions."

She plugged into her board, shook her head. "No response, sir. Not on any channel."

"Then continue to monitor all frequencies, Lieutenant." He paused a moment. Then he said to Sulu, "Phaser crews stand by, Mr. Sulu." He waited another moment before he added "Maintain yellow alert." He rose from his chair. "Mr. Spock, it's time."

Down in Engineering, still unknown, unheard, Kryton's disk made contact. The lights in the matter-antimatter grille flickered before they returned to full strength. Kirk, on deck five, was walking down the corridor to Elaan's cabin. As he'd expected, two guards stood at her door. But neither was Kryton. A little uneasy he said, "Where is Kryton?"

"On business," said a guard. Both lifted their weapons. "No one may enter the Dohlman's presence," one said.

"Inform her glory that Captain Kirk requests the honor of a visit."

"The Dohlman has said I shall be whipped to death if I let Captain Kirk pass through this door." Kirk pushed past them. The weapons leveled. A beam flashed twice. The guards fell; and Spock, phaser in hand, came out of the opposite door. "Have them taken to the Security Holding area, Mr. Spock."

Spock said, "Captain, how did you anticipate that she would deny you admittance? The logic by which you arrived at your conclusion escapes me."

"On your planet, Mr. Spock, females are logical. No other planet in the galaxy can make that claim."

He opened Elaan's door to see her sitting before a mirror. She was absorbed in combing the shining hair. As she saw his reflection in the glass, she flew to the bed where she'd discarded her belted dagger. Holding it high, she rushed at Kirk, its point at his heart. He seized her wrist and she shrieked, "You dare to touch a member of the royal family of Elas?"

"In self-defense, I certainly do." He removed the dagger and she tried to rake his face with her nails. He closed with her, holding her arms immobilized.

"For what you are doing the penalty is death on Elas!"

"You're not on Elas now. You are on my ship. I command here."

She bit his arm. The pain took him off guard. His hold on her loosened—and she was gone, fled into the adjoining bathroom, its door clicking locked behind her.

"That's your warning, Captain!" she called through it. "Don't ever touch me again!"

"All right," Kirk shouted in answer. "Then I'll send in Mr. Spock or Dr. McCoy! But I'll tell you one thing! You're going to do what you've been ordered to do by Councils, Tribunals and bureaucrats . . ."

He'd had it. A Klingon warship in the offing—and here he was, stuck behind a bathroom door trying to make sense to an overindulged brat who had no sense. "I'm leaving!" he yelled. "I'm through with you!"

She opened the door. "Captain . . ." She hesitated. "There . . . is one thing you . . . can teach me . . ."

"No, there isn't!" he roared at her. "You were right the first time! There's nothing I want to teach you! Not any more! You know everything!"

She began to cry. "I don't know everything. I don't know how to make people like me. Everybody hates me . . ."

He was startled into contrition. Genuine tears flooded the dark eyes. It was a sight he'd never thought to see. "Now look . . ." he said. "It's not that anybody hates you . . ."

"Yes, they do," she sobbed. "Everybody does . . ."

He went to her and wiped the tear-wet cheeks with his hand. "Stop crying," he said. "It's just that nobody likes to be treated as though they didn't exist . . ."

He was suddenly conscious of heat. "Something's wrong with the ventilation of this room . . . I—I need some air . . . we'll have a short recess, your glory."

"Captain . . ." He turned from the door. The luscious mouth was smiling at him, the pearl-toned arms outstretched to him. He stared at her for a long moment. Then he went straight into the arms. He kissed her— and the world, the Klingon ship, the High Commissioner, all he'd ever known in his life before was as though it had never existed.

She whispered, "You . . . slapped me."

Unsteadily, Kirk said, "We'll . . . talk about it later . . ."

His mouth found hers again.

Uhura, checking her dials, pushed the intercom button.

"Bridge to Captain," she said. She glanced over at Spock. "Mr. Spock, I'm getting—"

"I have it on my sensor," Spock said.

"Bridge to Captain," she repeated, frowning. "Come in, Captain. Captain Kirk, please answer."

Kirk's voice came, unfamiliar, dazed. "Kirk here."

"Captain, I'm picking up a transmission from inside the *Enterprise*. It's on a tight beam aimed at the Klingon vessel."

Elaan was nibbling at the lobe of Kirk's ear. "Transmission?" he echoed vaguely. Her lashes were black. They should have been silver blonde but they weren't. He said, "Stop that." She kissed the ear; and he was able to focus his attention on the intercom long enough to ask, "Can you pinpoint the source of the transmission, Lieutenant?"

"Spock here, Captain. I am triangulating now. It's coming from the engine room, sir."

The news broke through his entrancement. "Security to engineering! An intruder! Security alert all decks!"

He ran for the door and the elevator. In the engine room, Scott met him, his face stricken. He pointed to the body of Watson. "Watson must have discovered the devil after he'd sneaked in here. He got killed for it. He had this in his hand when I found him. It looks like some kind of transmitter."

Kirk took it. "It's Klingon," he said.

McCoy rose from Watson's body. "Neck snapped clean, Jim."

Kirk walked over to where two Security guards, their phasers trained on Kryton, held the ape-jawed Elasian in custody.

"What signal did you send that Klingon ship? What was your assignment?"

Impassive, his small eyes bright with scorn, Kryton said, "Captain, you must know I will say nothing. Our interrogation methods are far more excruciating than anything you people are capable of."

"I'm aware you're trained to resist any form of *physical* torture." Kirk moved to the intercom. "Kirk to Spock."

"Spock here, Captain."

"Mr. Spock, it is Kryton who's been transmitting. He refuses to talk. I'll need you to do the Vulcan mindmeld."

"Captain!" It was Evans, one of the Security guards. "The prisoner—he's sick . . ." Kirk whirled to see Kryton clutch at his stomach. The Elasian sagged at the knees—and his hand whipped out to seize Evans' phaser. He reversed it, fired it at himself and disappeared.

Stunned, Evans said, "Captain, I'm sorry. But he really seemed—"

"What was he hiding that was so important he had to die to keep it secret?" Hard-faced, Kirk turned to Scott. "He didn't come in here just to use a transmitter. Scotty, I want you to check every relay you've got."

"Captain, do you realize how many relays there are in Engineering?"

"Don't waste time telling me. Do it!"

He wasted no time himself in getting back to Elaan's cabin. She took the news of Kryton's suicide quietly. "He's been half out of his mind ever since the announcement of my wedding. He was of noble family—and he loved me."

"Then he sold out to the Klingons out of jealousy?"

"Probably." She laid her hand on his heart. "It is mine, is it not? Let us not speak of unimportant matters."

"There's a Klingon warship out there," he told her. "What is it there for? It isn't keeping pace with us just to prevent your marriage."

She put her silver blonde head on his shoulder. "We should welcome their help against the marriage," she said.

He grasped her upper arms. "Elaan, two planets, the stability of an entire star system depends on your marriage. We both have a duty to forget what happened."

"Could you do that? Give me to another man?"

"My orders—and yours—say you *belong* to that other man. What happened between us was an accident."

"It was no accident. I chose you and you chose me." Before he could speak, she added, "I have a plan. With

145

this ship you could utterly obliterate Troyius. Then there would be no need for the marriage. Our grateful people would give you command of the star system."

He stared at her in horror. "How can you think of such a monstrous thing?"

"He is Troyian," she said. And was in his arms again. "You cannot fight against this love . . . against my love."

"Captain!" It was Spock on the intercom. There was a pause before he said, "May we see you a moment?"

Kirk didn't answer. The witch in his arms was right. He could not fight against this love, this passion, this fatality—whatever it was, whatever name one chose to give it. Nameless or named, it held him in thrall. His lips were on hers again—and the door opened. Spock and McCoy stood there, staring in unbelief.

"Jim!"

Kirk raised unseeing eyes.

"Jim! May I have a word with you, please?"

Kirk pulled free of the clinging arms; and moved toward the door with the slow, ponderous walk of a man walking under water. He looked back at Elaan. Then he stumbled out into the corridor.

"Captain, are you all right?" Spock said.

He nodded.

"Jim, did she cry?"

"What?"

"Did she cry? Did her tears touch your skin?"

Kirk frowned. "Yes."

McCoy sighed. "Then we're in trouble. Jim, listen to me. Petri told Christine that Elasian women's tears contain a biochemical substance that acts like a super, grade A love potion."

Kirk was staring at the hand that had wiped the tears from Elaan's cheek. "And according to Petri, the effects don't wear off," McCoy said.

"Bones, you've got to find me an antidote."

"I can try but I'll need to make tests of—"

The corridor intercom spoke. "Bridge to Captain!"

"Kirk here."

Sulu's anxious voice said, "Captain, the Klingon ship

146

has changed course! It's heading toward us at warp speed!"

All look of bemusement left Kirk's face. "Battle stations!" he ordered crisply. "I'm on my way."

Klaxon alarm shrieks filled the bridge as he stepped from the elevator. A fast glance at the screen showed the swiftly enlarging image of the Klingon ship. "Stand by, phasers!" he ordered, running to his command chair.

"Phasers ready, sir," Sulu reported.

Spock called, "His speed is better than Warp Six, Captain!"

Eyes on the screen, Kirk said, "Mr. Chekov, lay in a course to take us clear of this system. If he wants to fight, we'll need room to maneuver."

"Course computed, sir," Chekov said.

"And laid in, Captain."

"Very well, Mr. Sulu. Ahead, Warp Two and—"

The intercom beeped to the sound of Scott's agitated voice. "Captain! The matter-anti-matter reactor is—"

Before Scott had uttered the next word, Kirk had barked, "Belay that order, Mr. Sulu!"

Sulu jerked his hand from the button he was about to push as though it were red-hot. Spock left his station to come and stand beside Kirk.

"What is it, Scotty?"

Everyone on the bridge could hear Scott say, "The anti-matter pod is rigged to blow up the moment we go into warp drive."

Moments went by before Kirk spoke. Then he said, "That bomb he planted, Scotty. Can you dismantle it?"

"Not without blowing us halfway across the galaxy."

Like a blow Kirk could feel the pressure of the eyes focussed on him. He drew a deep breath. "Then give us every ounce of power you've got from the impulse drive. And find a solution to that bomb."

It was into this atmosphere of repressed excitement that Elaan stepped from the bridge elevator. On the screen the Klingon ship was growing in size and detail. "Mr. Sulu, stand by to make your maneuvers smartly. She'll be sluggish in response."

Kirk turned back to the screen and saw Elaan. Absorbed though he was in crisis, he had to fight the impulse to go to her by grasping the arms of his chair. Spock moved closer to him; and Sulu said tonelessly, "One hundred thousand kilometers."

Time ambled by. Then Sulu said, "Ninety kilometers."

"Hold your fire," Kirk said.

Sulu moistened his lips. "Sixty. Fifty."

On the screen the Klingon ship blurred in a burst of speed. "She's passed us without firing a shot," Sulu said very quietly.

"Captain, I don't think they meant to attack us," Spock said. Now that the crisis had passed, Kirk was conscious again only of the presence of Elaan. He rose from his chair as though pulled to her by an invisible chain. Watchful, Spock said warningly, "*This* time we have been fortunate."

The invisible chain snapped. Kirk sank back in his chair. "Yes, their tactics are clear now. They were trying to tempt us to cut in warp drive. That way we'd have blown ourselves up. Their problem would have been solved for them without risking war with the Federation. Very neat."

"Very," Spock said. "But why do they consider the possession of this system so vital?"

"A very good question, Mr. Spock."

"I have another question, sir. Isn't the bridge the wrong place for the Dohlman to be at a time like this?"

"I'll be the judge of—" Kirk began. He met Spock's eyes. "You're right, Mr. Spock. Thank you."

He strode over to Elaan. "I want you to leave the bridge and go to Sickbay. It's the best-protected part of the ship."

"I want to be with you," she said.

"Your presence here is interfering with my efficiency —my ability to protect you."

"I won't go."

Gripping her shoulders, he propelled her toward the elevator. Over her head, he looked at Spock. "You have the con, Mr. Spock."

As the elevator door slid closed, she flung her arms about his neck. "I love you. I have chosen you. But

I do not understand why you did not fight the Klingon."

"If I can do better by my mission by running away, then I run away."

"That mission," she said, "is to deliver me to Troyius."

"Yes, it is," he said.

"You would have me wear my wedding dress for another man and never see me again?"

"Yes, Elaan."

"Are you happy at that prospect?"

"No."

The intercom buzzed. "Scott to Captain."

"Kirk here."

"Bad news, Skipper. The entire dilythium crystal converter assembly is fused. No chance of repair. It's completely unusable."

"No way to restore warp drive?"

"Not without the dilythium crystal, sir. We can't even generate enough power to fire our weapons."

"Elaan, I've got to get back to the bridge. *Please* go to Sickbay. There's its door. Down this corridor."

She stood on tiptoe to kiss his forehead. "Yes, my brave love."

He watched her move down to the Sickbay door. Whatever chemical substance it was in the tears he had wiped from her cheek, it was powerful stuff.

Mysteriously baffling was how McCoy was finding it. Twenty-four tests—and analysis of it was as elusive as ever.

Petri watched him examine a read-out handed him by Nurse Christine. "You're wasting your time," he said. "There is no antidote to the poison of Elasian tears. The men of Elas have tried desperately to locate one. They've always failed." He had leaned back against his pillow when Elaan opened the Sickbay door. She addressed McCoy. "The Captain asked me to come here for safety."

Petri raised his head again. "And our safety? What about that with this woman around? How do you estimate our chances for survival, Dr. McCoy?"

"That's the Captain's responsibility," McCoy said.

Petri looked soberly thoughtful. After a long moment, he reached down into the gold casket he'd placed under his bed and withdrew the necklace Elaan had rejected. He pulled on his robe and walked slowly over to her.

"I have failed in my responsibility to my people," he said heavily. "With more wisdom I might have been able to prepare you to marry our ruler. Now that we may all die, I again ask you to accept this necklace as a token of respect for the true wish of my—of our people—for peace between us."

"Responsibility, duty—that's all you men ever think about!" she said angrily.

But she took the necklace.

When Kirk got back to the bridge, it was for more bad news. It was Uhura who had to give it to him. "A message from the Klingon ship, sir. We are ordered to stand by for boarding or be destroyed. They demand an immediate reply."

"So he's going to force a fight," Kirk said.

Back in his command chair, he struck his intercom button. "Kirk to Engineering. Energy status, Scotty?"

"Ninety-three percent of impulse power, Captain."

"We can still maneuver, sir," Spock said.

"Aye, we can wallow like a garbage scow," Scott said. "Our shields will hold out for a few passes. But without the matter-anti-matter reactors, we've no chance against a starship. Captain, can't you call Starfleet in *this* emergency?"

"And tell the Klingons they've succeeded in knocking out the warp engines?" Kirk retorted. "No, we'll stall for time."

He swung around to confront the taut faces in the bridge. "We will proceed," he said, "on course; in hope that the Klingons can be bluffed—or think better of starting a general war. Lieutenant Uhura, open a hailing frequency."

He seized his speaker. "This is Captain James Kirk of the *USS Enterprise* on Federation business. Our mission is peaceful but we are not prepared to accept interference."

The hoarse Klingon voice filled the bridge. "Prepare to be boarded or destroyed."

"Very effective, our strategy," Kirk muttered.

"Captain, the Klingon is closing in on an intercept course!" Sulu exclaimed. "Five hundred thousand kilometers." He added, "Deflector shields up!"

It was the moment Elaan chose to step out of the bridge elevator, radiant in the shimmering white of her wedding dress, the Troyian necklace of pellucid jewels around her neck. Kirk tore his eyes from the vision she made—and hit the intercom with his fist. "Mr. Scott, can you deliver even partial power to the main phaser banks?"

"No, sir. Not a chance."

Elaan was beside Kirk. Averting his eyes from her, he said, "I told you to stay in Sickbay."

"If I'm going to die, I want to die with you."

"We don't intend to die. Leave the bridge."

She drifted away toward the elevator and stopped to lean her head back against the wall.

Sulu shouted, "One thousand kilometers!"—and the ship shuddered under impact by a Klingon missile. As it burst against a deflector shield, its flash bathed the *Enterprise* in a multi-colored auroral light.

"He's passed us," Spock said. "All shields held."

"Mr. Sulu, come to 143 mark 2. Keep our forward shields to him."

"Here he comes again, sir," Sulu said.

"Stay with the controls. Keep those forward shields to him." On the screen the Klingon ship was an approaching streak of speed.

"He's going for our flank, Mr. Sulu. Hard over! Bring her around!"

The force of the second missile shook every chair in the bridge. "Sulu!" Kirk shouted.

"Sorry, Captain. She won't respond fast enough on impulse drive."

"He's passed us again," Spock said. "There's damage to number four shield, sir."

"How bad?"

"It won't take another full strike. Captain, I'm getting some very peculiar readings on the sensor board."

151

"What sort of readings, Mr. Spock?"

The Vulcan had seized his tricorder and was scanning the bridge area with it. Suddenly, he leaped from his chair to point to Elaan. *"She* is the source!" he cried.

"She?" Kirk said. "You mean Elaan?"

"The necklace, Captain!"

Both men ran to her. "What kind of jewels are in that thing?" Kirk demanded.

Bewildered, she fingered the necklace. "We call the white beads radans. They are quite common stones."

Spock scanned the diamonds with a circular device on his tricorder. Under it, they glowed and sparkled with an unearthly fire.

"It's only because of its antiquity that the necklace is prized," Elaan said.

"Common stones!" Kirk said. "No wonder the Klingons are interested in this star system! May I have that necklace, your glory?"

"If it can be of any help—of course," she said.

"You may just have saved our lives," Kirk said. "Mr. Spock, do you think Scotty could use some dilithium crystals?"

"There's a highly positive element in your supposition, Captain." The necklace in hand, Spock entered the elevator.

"He's coming in again, sir," Sulu cried.

"Mr. Sulu, stand by my order to turn *quickly* to port. Try to protect number four shield. *Now,* Mr. Sulu! Hard to port!"

Again the shields reflected the brilliant interplay of multi-colored light as the ship vibrated under shock by the Klingon attack. "Shields holding but weakened," Sulu called.

"Captain, message coming in," Uhura reported. At Kirk's nod, she hit the speaker.

The guttural Klingon voice had triumph in it. *"Enterprise,* our readings confirm your power extremly low, your shields buckling. This is your last chance to surrender."

Sulu said, "Number four shield just collapsed, sir. Impulse power down to 31 percent."

152

Kirk walked over to Uhura's station. "Lieutenant, open a channel." He seized the microphone. "This is Captain Kirk. I request your terms of surrender."

"No terms. Surrender must be unconditional and immediate."

Kirk struck the intercom button. "Scotty, what's the estimate?"

"We're fitting it now, sir. We'll need to run a few tests to make sure—"

"We'll test it in combat."

Spock said, "Those are crude crystals, sir. There's no way to judge what the unusual shapes will do to energy flow."

Scott used the intercom to add his caution. "Captain, a hitch in the energy flow could blow us up just as effectively as—"

Kirk cut him off. "Let me know when it's in place." He returned to Uhura. "Hailing frequency again, Lieutenant." Back at his command chair, he said into his speaker, "This is the *USS Enterprise*. Will you guarantee the safety of our passenger, the Dohlman of Elas?"

The harsh voice repeated, "No conditions. Surrender immediate."

"Captain, he's starting his run!"

"I see, Mr. Sulu." Standing before the screen, Kirk felt a quiet hand laid on his arm. Elaan watched with him as death in the form of the Klingon ship neared them, itself a black missile made vague by speed. Then Scott spoke from the intercom. "It's in place, sir—but I can't answer for . . ."

"Get up here fast!" Kirk said. He wheeled from the screen. "Mr. Sulu, stand by for warp maneuver. Mr. Chekov, arm photon torpedoes."

"Photon torpedoes ready, sir."

"Warp power to the shields, Captain?"

"Negative, Mr. Sulu. His sensors would pick up our power increase. The more helpless he thinks we are, the closer he'll come. It's as he passes I want warp drive cut in. You'll pivot at Warp Two, Mr. Sulu, to bring all tubes to bear."

"Aye, sir."

"Mr. Chekov, give him the full spread of photon torpedoes."

Scott rushed into the bridge to take his place at his station and Sulu said, "One hundred thousand kilometers, sir."

"Mr. Scott, stand by to cut in warp power."

The engineer looked up from his control. "Fluctuation, Captain. It's the shape of the crystals. I was afraid of that."

"Seventy-five kilometers," Sulu said.

"He'll fire at minimum range, Mr. Sulu."

"Forty," Sulu said.

Scott's worried eyes were on the flickering lights of his board. "It won't steady down, Captain."

The mass of the Klingon ship nearly filled the screen. Kirk said, "Warp in, Scotty. Full power to the shields. Mr. Sulu, warp two. Come to course 147 mark 3."

The Klingon ship fired. The *Enterprise* swerved, began to rotate dizzily in the dazzle of the now familiar auroral blaze reflected from its wounded shields.

"We're still here!" Scott cried, unbelieving.

"Fire photon torpedoes! Full spread!"

They waited. Elaan's hand found Kirk's. Then it came. From far out in space there came the shattering roar of explosion, of tearing metal. Another one detonated.

"Direct hit amidship by photon torpedo!" Sulu yelled.

Spock lifted his head. "Damage to Klingon number three shield, Captain. Number four obliterated. They've lost maneuver power, sir."

Chekov turned. "He's badly damaged. Retreating at reduced speed, sir."

"Secure from general quarters," Kirk said.

Elaan, her eyes shining with proud excitement, looked at him, startled. "You will not pursue and finish him off?"

"No." His eyes met hers. It was a long moment before he was able to say, "Mr. Sulu, resume course to Troyius."

Having said it, he looked away from the dead hope in her face.

In the Transporter Room, Petri had taken his place on the platform. As Elaan entered in her wedding dress, she touched the Troyian necklace she wore and smiled at him. "The two missing stones in this," she said, "saved all our lives, Ambassador Petri." He bowed deeply.

She went to Kirk. "You will beam-down for—the ceremony?"

"No."

She detached the jeweled dagger from her belt. "I wish you to have this as a personal memento. You have taught me that such things are no longer for me." She stooped and kissed his hand. "Remember me," she whispered.

"I have no choice," he said.

"Nor have I. All we've got now is duty and responsibility."

She took her place on the platform, her two guards beside her. "Good-bye, Captain James Kirk." Her voice broke.

"Good-bye," Kirk said. He walked swiftly to Scott at the transporter desk. "Energize," he said. Scott turned the dial and the figure of Elaan began to shimmer. He turned for his last look at her. Her eyes were on his, bright with tears.

McCoy met him excitedly as he walked out of the bridge elevator. "Jim, I've finally isolated the poisonous substance in that woman's tears. I think I've found the antidote."

"There's no need for it, Doctor," Spock said. "The Captain has found his own antidote. The *Enterprise* infected the Captain long before the Dohlman's tears touched him."

Kirk said, "Mr. Sulu, take us out of orbit. Ahead Warp Two."

Was the *Enterprise* the antidote to Elaan? McCoy and Spock seemed very sure it was. He was not so sure. Not now, anyway.

PSYCHIC WORLD

Here are some of the leading books that delve into the world of the occult—that shed light on the powers of prophecy, of reincarnation and of foretelling the future.

☐ **THE SEARCH FOR THE GIRL WITH THE BLUE EYES** by Jess Stearn. The story of a young woman's reincarnation. (N4591—95¢)

☐ **PSYCHIC PEOPLE** by Eleanor Touhey Smith. The revealing account of 19 men and women with strange and supernatural powers. (N4471—95¢)

☐ **EDGAR CAYCE: THE SLEEPING PROPHET** by Jess Stearn. The bestselling study of the late mystic's prophecies and astounding readings. (Q6764—$1.25)

☐ **A GIFT OF PROPHECY** by Ruth Montgomery. The phenomenal account of Jeane Dixon's uncanny ability to forsee the future. (N4223—95¢)

☐ **YOGA, YOUTH AND REINCARNATION** by Jess Stearn describes the skeptical author's experience with the ancient art of yoga. (Q6508—$1.25)

☐ **THE COMPLETE BOOK OF PALMISTRY** by Joyce Wilson. A step-by-step fully-illustrated course in the ancient art of reading palms. (P5689—$1.00)

☐ **PSYCHIC DISCOVERIES BEHIND THE IRON CURTAIN** by Sheila Ostrander & Lynn Schroeder. Reports of government sponsored research on artificial reincarnation, astrological birth control and other psychic phenomena. Fully documented discoveries. (Q6581—$1.25)